Neil Eccles is a father and linguist with a flawed personality and an obtuse view on people, literature and music. He particularly enjoys running on the fells, listening to music, reading 19th and 20th century French literature and watching people in pubs.

He is 48 and this is his first book. He has no idea what he is doing, in writing this book or in life generally.

To Millie, Maddie and Eddie.

Neil Eccles

THE VITUPERATION OF DR DEREK RAMSBOTTOM

AUSTIN MACAULEY PUBLISHERS™

LONDON • CAMBRIDGE • NEW YORK • SHARJAH

A CIP catalogue record for this title is available from the British Library.

ISBN 9781787104075 (Paperback)
ISBN 9781787104082 (E-Book)

www.austinmacauley.com

First Published (2018)
Austin Macauley Publishers Ltd™
25 Canada Square
Canary Wharf
London
E14 5LQ

Acknowledgements

I would like to thank Gareth, lifelong friend, for his faith in me and for taking the time to read the original manuscript. I love you, man. Boys *do* cry after all.

I would like to thank my family. You breathe my air and bleed my blood.

I would like to thank the pub-dwellers and café-crawlers of Leeds. Inspiration is necessarily intangible. You don't know who you are and neither do I but without you there would be no book.

I would like to thank all those musicians and lyricists whose works have invaded my life and who have created something from nothing. If you hear or see yourself in this book, please accept my thanks for pervading my existence.

I would like to thank Mr Tosounidis, Trauma and Orthopaedic Surgeon at Leeds General Infirmary. You saved my life. Truly you did. I owe you more than I could ever repay.

I would like to thank my publishers. I may be just one more writer. But without you I wouldn't even be that.

Disclaimer

Synopsis

We all like to play innocent. But no one is innocent. No one. So does that make us all guilty? Probably.

A fatal car accident in a residential area close to a large, red-brick university. To the Emergency Services, a simple case of a skint, carefree and doped student running out of fuel at a busy junction.

But why do five ostensibly decent, upstanding and intelligent people, who are primary witnesses to the accident, walk away from the scene?

How could two of them, who know the victim well, turn their backs and disappear into the night?

This is a crude and abrasive journey into the world of education, in which knowledge and intellect lead not to a greater understanding of the world around us but to a deeper frustration at the absence of meaning in our existence.

Education is pointless. Love is pointless. Existence is pointless. Words are pointless. This book is pointless.

And Dr Derek Ramsbottom is but an innocent bystander. Literally and figuratively.

Well, not quite.

Epilogue

At the moment the car mounts the curb, Robert Smith is screaming at her to get it out, to get it out, to get her fucking voice out of his head.

His wailing is so desperate that she doesn't hear the engine of the shit-brown Honda Civic cut out at full tilt, she doesn't hear her name bellowed repeatedly through the sodden trees and she doesn't hear the trainers screeching across the damp tarmac to reach her.

She doesn't see the driver crying at the wheel as the Civic rears up at her, she doesn't see her lover lumbering forlornly through the park-side playground towards her and she doesn't see her stalker lunging desperately to rugby-tackle her clear.

She doesn't see because she has closed her eyes. Robert Smith has called her into his world and she is nowhere else.

Robert never wanted this, he never wanted any of this. He wishes her dead. He wishes her dead.

She is completely beholden to him. She is not at the bus stop on Highcliffe Corner. She is not waiting for her lover to turn up late again so that she can tell him to fuck off once and for all. She is not ignoring the autistic, spindly stalker, who has been running down the hill towards her for the last five minutes or more. She is not wondering why an interfering old man with a sniffy old sheepdog is hovering in the trees in anticipation for the third time in as many weeks. She is not about to be hit by a familiar, battered old car as her drug supplier swerves clear only inches behind. And she is not about to be photographed by a wiry woman, brandishing a tablet in the central reservation of the dual carriageway.

Except.

Except that Robert Smith is not her Guardian Angel, he is not her Knight in Shining Armour, he is not her reality.

Robert Smith is the lead singer of The Cure. Robert Smith has spent over thirty years wearing make-up and oversized pumps, apparently hanging upside down like a bat while his hairpiece sets, trying to escape snake-pits and spiders' webs and existential humiliation, and writing lines about wild mood swings and funeral parties and the shallow-drowned. Robert Smith appears to have a very tenuous grip on his own reality, let alone someone else's.

So there will be no cure. There is no elsewhere. This is Highcliffe Corner just after last orders.

And by the time the body hits the concrete. And the bones crack. And the blood runs. And the hair mats. And the eyes roll. And the earphones split her ears. By the time it is limp, Robert has moved on.

His girl is falling down a lot, she is always falling again and again; and he's there trying to catch her, but he doesn't even manage to catch her name.

She has fallen. Of that there is no doubt. And the driver and the lover and the stalker and the drug dealer and the old man and the photographer are too late to catch her. And the dog most certainly isn't going to catch her, any more than Robert is.

But they know her name. They all know her name. Except Robert, of course, who doesn't manage to catch it. And the dog.

And yet nine and a half minutes later, when the sirens arrive and the Highcliffe inebriates gather round, they are all gone. There is no sign of any of them, except the driver and the dog, who are too busy getting their fucking voices out of Robert's head to bear witness. Robert's wish has come to pass. And they are gone.

She is gone.

In those final moments, she was shouted dead, willed away by Mr Robert Smith. And eyes closed, ears smothered in The

Cure, she neither saw nor heard it coming. And by the time Mr Smith came to try and catch her as she fell, she had gone.

By the time the blues and the yellows and the reds arrive with their flashing lights and their cutting tools and their stretchers and their oxygen masks, she has gone, carried off into the dark green night of Highcliffe Park.

Did anyone catch her? Did anyone catch her name?

Part 1
Thursday

Chapter 1

It's one minute after nine. It's been a humid, overcast day and the light isn't good. And from Prakesh's Kebab House, Jonny can only just see the library door. And even then, he cannot actually see the oak panels themselves but the interior light, setting the ornate glass against the obscured exterior.

He dare not take his eyes off the door for a second. It will take her less than a minute to exit, lock the door and disappear around the corner. And in her skintight black 501s, chained, leather jacket and knee-length Dr. Martens, she'll be camouflaged. And she'll be gone.

'You buyin anyfin, mate?'

'Err, yes, ermm, just a lemonade, please.'

'Sprite ok for yer? Nuffin to eat?'

'No, thanks.'

'That'll be a pound, please, mate.'

'A quid? For a can?'

'Look, mate. You need to give me a pound or you're gonna be leaving. You've sat 'ere for ten minutes without buyin anyfin as it is. We're not a soup kitchen, fucksake.'

Jonny docs not take his eyes off the library, compounding Prakesh Junior's irritation. He slams the can down on the formica and slides the change into his hands, returning then to his stool behind the counter to watch MMA.

Jonny watches. She's late. It must be audit night. She's only ever late on audit night. Once a month. When they do a stock check or prepare the debt-letters.

The borrowers are mainly students. Students who forget who they are, who are not at all sure that they are alive, who sometimes even lose the will to stay alive, so they are not going to worry about a couple of inconsequential tomes on the 1926 General Strike or Applied Mechanics, are they? She sends out a lot of letters. A lot.

Jonny knows all this. Jonny knows all this because Jonny is special. He knows he is special. He must be. Because everyone says he is. Because, at school, all the teachers are very lovely to him. Even when he shouts out, or throws things, or cries, or walks out of class pushing desks out of his way. Because he has special lessons after school with Dr Ramsbottom and Ms Wilhelm.

He knows other people who have special lessons with Dr Ramsbottom or Ms Wilhelm. But not both. Only he has lessons with both. Sometimes he even comes in on a Saturday. When no one else is there. Just him. And Ms Wilhelm. Never Dr Ramsbottom on a Saturday. But Ms Wilhelm, yes.

Jonny wishes Dr Ramsbottom would come in on a Saturday instead. He is lovely. And kind. And he smiles lots. And he brings him sweets. And he never gets angry. And he shows him properly what to do. But he never gives him the answers. He says that Jonny is clever and that he should work it out for himself and that he wants him to be able to do it on his own. And that he is not an idiot.

Ms Wilhelm is not the same. She has never called him an idiot. But she is not the same.

She scares him. Jonny doesn't really understand why she scares him. But she does. And he tells his brother Sean that she makes him uncomfortable in his own skin. He doesn't really know what that means but he has heard Dr Ramsbottom say it in The Optic and he likes the words. And it makes Sean laugh and then Sean talks to him more.

He likes it when Sean talks to him more. Because normally Sean seems to get tired of waiting for him to say something and ends up texting in front of him or turning to talk to someone else. And these days he is always working at The Optic and there is always someone else to talk to. So he doesn't really talk to Jonny much anymore. But when Jonny uses clever words, Sean talks to him. So Jonny listens to Dr Ramsbottom and his grandad in the pub and he copies what they say.

Sometimes they laugh at him and he doesn't know why. So he laughs along with them and everyone is happy and Jonny likes it when everyone is happy. But sometimes they don't. Sometimes they look at him like he's just broken Grandma's best china mug and he gets a bit frightened, so he cries and says sorry. Grandma is not here anymore.

And when he cries, Grandad always comes and sits him down next to him in Curmudgeon Corner and lets him help put letters on The Board. That's what they call it because Grandad always sits there. Except on a Friday night, when lots of young people come in and they wear silly clothes and get very loud and Grandad sits at the end of the bar and talks to Dr Ramsbottom.

Grandad doesn't like it when the noisy people are in because he can't spread his Scrabble board out and he has to use a mini-board at the bar and he says it's like trying to think in a state of inebriation.

Jonny likes that phrase too. He shouts to Grandad, he shouts 'Are the noisy people in a state of inebriation, Grandad?' right across the bar. And this time they all laugh lots and Jonny is very, very happy.

Grandad puts letters down and the word is HYSTERICALLY and Jonny likes that word but Grandad says it is not very high-scoring and a bit of a waste of letters and he harrumphs.

Grandad harrumphs a lot.

He harrumphs very deeply when Jonny tells him about the help Ms Wilhelm is giving him and that she is making him come in on a Saturday morning. He is so angry that he tells Dr Ramsbottom and Dr Ramsbottom and Grandad have a long chat for a long time and they seem to be getting very annoyed. Not with one another. They do this a lot. Getting angry with nobody and nothing. Sometimes Grandad even swears. Grandad never swears.

And when they get annoyed, they drink more. It's like all the shouting is making them thirsty and Dr Ramsbottom pulls more and more pints and Grandad talks about the old days a lot and about how they made him leave and how he was pushed out and how the new world of teaching is feckless.

That word sounds rude to Jonny and he hears it again. Lots. Especially when the boy with the green jumper comes in when England are playing rugby. But without the 'less' on the end.

It is after one of these angry conversations that Grandad shows Jonny how to record on his mobile phone and how to keep it on when he is talking to people at school. But without them seeing. In his pocket. Especially Ms Wilhelm.

So when he is at school, he keeps it on and then Grandad gives it to Dr Ramsbottom to listen to and then they talk a lot about bad things. They use words like disingenuous and inappropriate and coercion. But Jonny doesn't really know what they are talking about. But they also use words like corruption and cheating. And Jonny does understand what they are. At least, he thinks he does.

Sometimes the phone runs out of battery and it makes Dr Ramsbottom cross because he cannot tell what happens and Grandad has to take Jonny to his corner and they think of another word for the Scrabble board. Jonny never thinks of a word. But Grandad sometimes thinks of one and then they pretend that Jonny thought of it. It makes Grandad smile again and Jonny likes it when Grandad smiles. He doesn't like it when Grandad is shouting and angry.

He doesn't really like it when they talk about the mobile phone business either but it is Grandad who asks him so it must be a good thing because Grandad is a nice man. He has a dog. A lovely sheepdog. So he must be a nice man.

There she is.

Jonny waits a matter of seconds and leaves the can, barely touched, on the table.

Just as she turns up Park Road and away from him, he exits the shop and walks calmly across the road. Just the odd screeching student car at this time, so he doesn't lose sight of her. Not that it matters particularly. He knows exactly where she is headed.

It's an easy pursuit. The tree-lined avenue affords him some shelter from the street-lighting, allowing him to walk in the shadows and avoid her occasional glance back.

But she doesn't need to turn her head to know that he is there. He has been doing it for weeks, same day same time. She leaves the library, she goes to Pete's to get her weed, she smokes a quick joint with Pete and passes the time and then she heads off back to Highcliffe Corner to meet her dad. And Jonny watches the whole journey, until she gets into the car at the bus stop.

She sometimes wonders what he does thereafter. But not for long.

The Doc drives, they walk, they talk about everything except the white elephant. He loosens her clothes. She unzips his trousers. She gives him an orgasm. He gives her one. Or maybe not. They go for a pint, he tells her he loves her without waiting for her to reciprocate. They walk a bit more, he drives.

And she gets out of his car wishing she had said never again. And he drives away wondering why she does not hang on his every literary reference, like she used to. And wondering if her muted gasp was faked or real.

But tonight, Jonny sees more.

He has long ago worked out why she goes to the first house. Jonny isn't stupid. He has seen the dodgy people coming and going from the house as he has watched it. The blinged up kit-cars, the expensive street clothes – Fila, Ellesse, Henri Lloyd, the constant attention to the phone screen, even whilst parking, the furtive side to sides peeping out the hoodies. And the discarded sealy bags dotted around the bins.

And she always comes out with an inane grin on her face, like the guilty schoolchild who has almost got away with another petty misdemeanour.

He doesn't like it. He doesn't like it at all. The thought that someone else, someone dodgy, might have influence over her movements, her personality.

And tonight Jonny notices a light on in the room adjacent to the kitchen, on the first floor. And he notices that the cheap, white blind on its window silhouettes any movement very clearly. And he notices that, after she has been there about twenty minutes, someone, a female, appears in silhouette in the room. He knows it's a female because he sees the arms unhinging the bra and he sees the erect nipples perfectly drawn out by the angled street light just outside the window.

And then he sees two people enjoying close contact. The sort of contact that leaves nothing to the imagination. It is not the sort of intercourse you see in films. It is not perfectly synergised, swaying and flailing bodies, tongues on skin and lordotic hip movements. It does not end with two faces arching away from one another, forcing the lower bodies together in a thrust of animal instinct.

It is her sitting on the edge of the bed and taking his manhood in her mouth. And then he turning her over and forcing his way into her too hastily. And it doesn't last more than ten minutes. She lurches forward and lies flat. He moves out of shot and appears in the kitchen moments later, spliff in hand. And ten minutes later, she walks out, looking not remotely dishevelled but slightly red in the cheek.

Jonny can tell that the freckles are up and he wishes he could get closer. Jonny loves freckles. But he is glad he can't. He is glad because he feels like a deceived husband, he feels like she has just adulterated their relationship, he feels like she is sneering at him and that the bloke inside is looking down at him now, laughing, laughing out loud.

And he is angry. And he feels violent. And he thinks of Saffi and Mum and he hates himself for even thinking it. Thinking that he could draw his arm up to a woman. Or anyone, for that matter. And Jonny runs. Jonny runs into the darkness of the park. He runs and runs. But he cannot run from himself. He cannot hide from his own conscience. He cannot right the wrongs in his mind. And he cannot unravel the labyrinth of filth twisting inside his head.

He fuckin hates himself. And now he is breathless, wheezy, bereft. He sits on the roundabout on Highcliffe Corner, legs dangled over the edge, gently turning it as he tries to stop the tears eking out of his eyes and rolling down his face. And he doesn't know how long he is there. Ten minutes, twenty, maybe an hour. And then a shadow flickers through the trees at about fifty yards. She is moving briskly, furiously, desperately, as though she knows she is late but is angry to have to rush, as though she doesn't really want to get there at all.

Jonny is not frightened. Jonny knows exactly who it is.

And he wonders if her dad knows that she walks alone through the park late at night. And he wonders how she explains that she wants picking up two hours after the library shuts. And he wonders why her dad would be picking her up at all when she is at university. And he wonders how she hides the smell of pot and sex from him. And he wonders if Dad has any inclination of the danger she is in.

And Jonny resolves to approach the car one day soon and lean in around her as she gets in, to tell Dad of her deviances.

Chapter 2

Beany sits on the stone step outside the front door, drawing on a rolly. It's one he skinned earlier whilst walking home from The Optic and it's a bit shit really – loose, damp, irritatingly acerbic on the tongue. Maybe it's the shot of Bourbon he had before he knocked off. His palate is numb.

It's a balmy evening after the earlier heavy rain and he wishes he'd lifted a couple of cans of cider on the way out.

He hasn't, of course. He wouldn't. He couldn't. Well, he could because the Doc is oblivious most of the time. But he's given his mum enough to worry about over the years without getting sacked, thrown off his course and banged up for theft. Besides, he hasn't been working at The Optic long and if he fucks up, he is putting his grandad in a tight spot in front of the Doc. Not to mention Jonny, whose world would collapse if he finds out that Sean is not the perfect human being.

And in any case, he likes the Doc.

The Doc is completely beaten down and smothered by the idiocy of the world around him – his job is an endless litany of excuses for failure, his wife is an endless litany of excuses for avoiding him whilst spending his money, and he lurches from one deception to another, his childlike idealism constantly disappointed by the humdrum inadequacies of daily reality.

But he retains an intellectual curiosity, a wry, sardonic humour and an avuncular warmth towards his customers, who are mostly young students just out for a laugh. He seems to welcome the vibrancy of their bawdy lust for life. It takes him away from his own life and feeds a nostalgia for his salad days, whatever and whenever they were.

Moreover, he has developed a genuine affection for Mafe and his dog. He can be very protective of the old boy: watching over him when other punters have a little dig at him; making sure Curmudgeon Corner is always free for him, even if the bar is packed; tidying up the Scrabble for him when he falls asleep over the last few squares, as he invariably does; insisting on pulling his pint of dark n mild himself, so that it is just right. So that the old boy doesn't finally realise that the Younger's is long gone.

And when the Doc realised that Jonny is Mafe's grandson, he started to look out for him at school and keep a discreet eye on his friendships, the classes he is put in and the teachers who teach him.

And recently, he dug Beany out of a little financial hole he had got himself into after going on a bit of drug bender and ending up owing a fistful of notes to his dealer. Not that Beany has ever met the bloke – Gareth looks after all that.

Beany, all of a sudden, needed an income and Mafe brought him in to meet the Doc, whose interview technique involved asking him to apron up sharpish and do a couple of hours behind the bar, there and then. Which Beany duly did and it became obvious pretty quickly that he knew his lager from his bitter and, even more impressive, his Keats from his Coleridge. The Doc hired him on the spot and even notched 20p an hour onto the 'advertised' rate… not that the Doc ever did any advertising.

Mrs Doc was livid when she found out about the extra 20p. But then she met Beany. And she soon went back to her café luncheons and her cosmetics evenings.

And so Beany wouldn't slip a couple of ciders into his bag on the end of a shift. He wouldn't undermine a man already struggling for reason and purpose. Sean Hainsworth is grateful for the job. Sean Hainsworth is grateful for the 20p extra. Sean Hainsworth is grateful to the Doc. Sean Hainsworth isn't stupid. Sean Hainsworth isn't stupid at all.

He took a first in French Literature and is now reading for a PhD. His thesis is on Decadence and Dementia in French 19th Century Authors and he's loving it. But he's run out of money, the grants are about to dry up after three years and he is going to have to get a proper job and finish the PhD whilst working full time.

He's dreading it. He hates businessmen. And women, come to that.

He hates the pretence and the power and the affectation and the self-importance and the constant twatting on about conversion rates and profit margins and company car specs and the endless boasting about vacuous coups de grâce and the gluttony and the conspicuous consumption and the tailored uniform and the humourless, humorous ties and the speeding tickets and the club-class upgrades and and and and and.

But on the other hand, he's sick of being poor, of living in rags, of sponging money off housemates' parents and other randomers, of eating Jack Fulton's sausages and feeling vaguely sick after almost every shitty meal, of feeling guilty about buying a fuckin takeaway pizza on a Friday night, of coming home to a bombsite of a kitchen and a fridge full of nothing more substantial than cold air n a few ice cubes and a lounge putrid with the stench of stale sweat and rotting tins and musty wallpaper.

Fuck knows what's around the corner. But it would be nice to be smoking this joint instead of chewing it like The Man with No fuckin Name. Where's the fuckin Zippo, fucksake?

A window over the road slides open. Beany sees two workman's hands on the flaky paintwork and, just, the tensed biceps as he lifts the sash wide open. The light hides the face and Beany, like Gareth, ponders the identity of Musicman. He knows nothing of him. But he knows what's coming next.

It's Thursday night. Thursday night is Electronica night.

Every other night of the week, Musicman plays a range of music for which the word 'eclectic' is utterly inadequate. Last night he had Orchestral Post Rock, Swedish Techno, some kind of Bangla Hip Hop and what can only be described as Metal

Flamenco, all in the space of an hour. The bloke must spend all his money on music. And the funny thing is that no one ever complains. No one ever goes knocking at his door asking him to turn it down or turn it off or change the tune or whatever. Not even at 2 in the morning. And Beany and Gareth have become so intrigued by this guy's existence and music tastes that they have started posting requests through his letterbox to see if he'll play them.

Over 3 months they've been doing that. Nothing yet. Or at least, nothing they've heard. Maybe he's not getting the post-its, maybe he's just throwing them disdainfully into the bin. Maybe he's surreptitiously playing the tunes when they are not in, quietly curious but too proud to play music that someone else might have heard before him.

And now, finally, just as the whole bizarre post-it scenario has slipped from Beany's mind; just as he's bracing for another aural blast of unlistenable originality, he hears the unmistakeably austere, hollow, organic gizmology of Mr Martin Gore.

The haunting minimalism of the great Depeche Mode mop-top is invasive, insidious, unnerving. This is MG at his nihilistic best. If Nietzsche had written music in search of proof that God did not in fact exist in any form – quite counter to the lifelong beliefs of his father – then this would have been close. Indeed, the Electric Ladyboy Studio in which this virtually unnoticed release was recorded is in Germany. Though Beany would have to concede that it probably wasn't there when Nietzsche was doing his stuff. And probably the technology wasn't quite up to the job either…

Beany almost shouts out loud when he hears it. He picks up the mobile to tell Gareth but, just as he is about to hit the buttons, the phone rings anyway. It must be Gareth. It must be. Maybe he's a few doors away and has heard it. Fuckin 'ell this is great.

MUM
ACCEPT OR DECLINE
ACCEPT OR DECLINE

ACCEPT OR DECLINE

ACCEPT

'Hi, Mum. How's it goin?'

'Sean, Sean. Is Jonny with you?'

'No, Mum. Why would he be?'

'Oh fuck. Where is he? It's getting on midnight. He's always back well before now. D'you see him at the pub tonight?'

'Yeah but ee left pretty sharpish, Mum. It's always pretty busy on a Thursday and you know he doesn't like being in there when it's busy. He buggered off to the library early doors. He often goes on a Thursday anyway.'

'The library? What library?'

'The uni library. He goes there sometimes to revise for his re-sits. Didn't you know?'

'No. He's never said anything. In any case, how does he get in there, he's hardly uni material?'

'I lend him my student card – I'm working anyway and they never check the ID in there. He loves it.'

'I don't gerrit, Sean. He's been telling me he's been going to see you and Grandad at The Optic on a Thursday. He's been telling me that for weeks. I don't understand. Jonny doesn't lie. Why would he not tell me he was going to the library?'

'Dunno, Mum, we'll sort that later but meantime where the fuck is he?'

'That's what I rang you to find out.'

'Fucksake. No idea. Jesus. Ermm, ok, let me think. Sure he'll be ok. Gimme a few mins and I'll ring you back.'

'Ok.'

'And try not to worry, Mum. Jonny ain't gonna do owt daft, is ee?'

'Ok.'

Chapter 3

She knows he won't leave his wife.

She knows because they never do. Because it's easier not to. Because he gets it all this way. Because it'll cost him. Because the Law won't be too pleased. Because he says he will too often.

And because The Optic is his home.

She's waiting at a bus stop. Highcliffe Corner. Buses come and go. She steps back each time. But the occasional one still heaves to a halt and she has to stammer some random words to make him go away. She is not alone. There is a shadow on the swings. She knows. He knows. She knows he knows. He knows she knows. Rain taps away at the shelter. It stopped raining a while ago but the old oak is dense and proud. Jonny watches the slightest body motion. And the cars.

The Doc is late. He always is. And the rain means money. Money for a room. He'll moan. So it'll probably be the back of the car. Even if it clears up, the grass at Highcliffe Ridge will be damp. Still, fewer nosy dog walkers.

A few minutes go by. A car pulls into the bus stop. She angles herself in.

'Fancy a walk?'

'Yeh. That be lovely.'

He pulls out into the traffic. A quick glance in the driver-side mirror. A longer one at Ellie's voluptuous frame.

'What's got into you? You're cheery.'

'Just fancy stretching my legs.'

'Yes. Where?'

'Dunno. Shall we do the river, down by Wilsden range? It's quiet down there.'

'Yeah, lovely. The Brown Cow's down there. We could nip for a pint. She's always open late.'

'You want to?'

'Yeah, let's do that.'

The Doc can be sullen, stolid. But you wouldn't know it tonight. He's full of it. Even the usual, dull school-talk is flecked with a wry humour.

'She ever teach you?'

'Who?'

'Wilhelm. The dowdy German ironing board.'

'Huh, yes, GCSE Maths. That's a few years ago now, though.'

'Yeah? What do you remember?'

'Dull. Uninspiring. Humourless. Kept making mistakes in her board-work.'

'You passed though, didn't you?'

'What do you take me for? Of course. I got a nice, comfortable B.'

'She help you?'

'Not really. Mr Shapiro was better. She kept havin people in after school, though. All the time. Wally Ashton got a bloody A and he didn't know a fraction from a fart.'

Derek throws back his head and laughs heartily.

'Wally Ashton… mmm…. is he Billy Ashton's brother?'

'Dunno. I left three years ago but if he's ginger and thick as shit then probably. Wally was in on Saturday mornings and everything. He virtually lived in that bloody place. She must a been bribing him with something cos he fuckin hated school… he was so shit at Maths…'

'Mmm. That figures.'

'Huh. Nice play on words.'

'Huh, cleverer than I look.'

'Good job.'

He puts his hand on her knee. She likes it when he does that. The warmth is occasional. But it's lovely when he exudes.

'Can we go away?'

'Where?'

'Don't care. I just want peace, with you.'

'Perhaps. She's going to see her mother in a fortnight and she might stay over.'

'Perfect.'

'Who sorts The Optic, though?'

'If I find someone, will you take me to Prague?'

'Yes. If you find someone.'

'I do love you for your enthusiasm, D.'

'A pleasure.'

He's safe. She won't find anyone. And she knows he won't go anyway.

They walk. They hold each other close. They nearly take off their clothes. Someone appears down an adjacent path. They re-dress hurriedly. They go to the pub. They drink too much.

She is back at the bus stop. The oak is still letting rain slip through its leaves and onto the shelter. It must be 4 hours since it poured. Lovely night sky. She walks home, ponderous. She loves him. But she is not at all sure why or how. She always leaves him with a sense of transience. And she quietly promises herself that she will just drift away, out of his compass, not contact him. He is old. But she only ever thinks about it after they separate.

Chapter 4

Gareth opens his eyes. The door-slam has woken him. A messy brown pattern flecked with yellow. Or orange. His carpet or vomit? Or both? A sullied skirting board and a plug socket not quite flush to the wall. And a glass just over half-full of water. For a while he can't turn his head to focus on anything else. It's hanging awkwardly over the edge of the rather grubby sheets and his world, for now at least, is barely six inches off the floor. The water in the glass is slightly cloudy and every few seconds, a solitary bubble escapes its molecular prison and makes for the meniscus. Gareth counts 20 and wonders how long he's been staring. Will the bubble-release speed up over time? Or slow down? To say he is eager to find out is overstating his curiosity. But he wouldn't mind knowing.

The room is in semi-darkness and outside on the landing, darker still, the tap tap of Sean's bedroom door in the breeze is out of time with the drip drip of the shower. Beany never bloody turns the tap off properly. Fucksake. It's weird, though. The drip drip is almost perfectly in time with the bubbles in the glass. Or maybe Gareth's mind is playing tricks on him. Again. Synchronicity. Great track. There were two, in fact. Gareth remembers a line about the din of Rice Krispies and can't pinpoint it to Synchronicity 1 or 2. Another one of those lyrics by Sting which should be utterly shite but is quite funny in the song.

Gareth can hear music. Just. His sash window looks out onto Titus Place and Musicman, as Gareth and Beany have imaginatively christened him, is making his presence felt, and heard. Gareth is a bit obsessed with Musicman. And now he and Beany are listening for his every musical move – Hard House, Techno, RnB, Grime, Metal, Indie Goth, Rap, Bangra Rap, Electronica.

And one sultry evening, Gareth sits for almost an hour on the edge of his bed, listening to the stunning second piano concerto by Rachmaninov and within the hour has googled him and found out that he was a very tall, angular musician with an extraordinary finger-span, allowing him to devise a tidal music of immense scope and pathos.

Sometimes, the music is so loud that Gareth's floor shakes to the bass and it invades his every sense, not so much aural sculpture as cranial rupture. Sometimes, it is at that annoying volume at which the ear is teased into recognising a tune which, in fact, it does not recognise. And the notes run away, escaping the memory altogether. But not escaping the ear. And he keeps listening, hoping that a series of bars might release his mind, confirming either that he does not know it or that he definitively does. And never quite doing either.

But this is clear. It is loud and it is unmistakeable. Gareth loves PJ Harvey.

PJ Harvey has been nominated for a Mercury Music Prize countless times and she has won it. PJ Harvey is an angry, brooding, laconic guitarist with a face of the shy, slightly dangerous schoolgirl she probably was. And yet it is one of those faces. The more you look at it, the less you get a sense of the person behind it. It hides her. Just as she hides who she really is, apparently, by clinging to those initials, instead of telling us that she is just Polly. Polly Jean. If you were to get too close to Polly Jean Harvey, Gareth has the sense that she would either spit at you or kiss you so violently that your tongue would bleed for a week. And tonight she is ripping through *The Whores Hustle and the Hustlers Whore*, whose title alone presages the volcanic guitars, the stamping bass and the wailing voice.

The bloke at number 23 is either very bloody angry or he's going out on the pull. Either way, something is definitely not quite right. It is Thursday. It's always Electronica on a Thursday. But not this Thursday, it seems.

And the funny thing is, Gareth has never actually seen this bloke. His silhouette, yes. His range of townie clothes hanging from the curtain rail, yes. His limited edition Nike boots airing on the sill, yes. His dirty mountain bike hanging from the bedroom ceiling, yes. Even his girlfriend has occasionally come to breathe smoke out of the flaky window, usually without much material between her flesh and the chancing glance of the neighbours. Or any at all. It occurs to Gareth that he doesn't even know if this bloke is Black, White, Asian or Mixed. No idea. It also occurs to him that there was a time when music would put you in a social, intellectual and even racial box. Not anymore. And it occurs to Gareth that if someone were to ask him to name one beautiful thing about the modern world, it would be music. Music. Because it is simply unfathomable. It is like diving into the deepest ocean – it smothers and threatens to suffocate but its vibrancy attacks and attaches to your entire sentient consciousness and you cannot escape it. You do not want to escape it. It becomes you.

And Gareth finally loses count of the bubbles, draws his head away from the shitty carpet and lies back on the pillow. Beany's rattling door is annoying him. But if he shuts out the draft, he shuts out the music. Fucksake. So he lies there. And he lies there. And he lies there. How long, he doesn't know. But long enough for 85 bubbles to rise to the surface. That he does know. Because the shower tap has dripped 85 times. Fucksake. He gets up and shuts the door. But the moment has now gone. That state of catharsis in which the sights and the smells and the sounds of the vicinity flow over him, through him and become his vision and his odour and his noise. It has passed. Standing upright, even momentarily, is too much. His phone buzzes. Text.

'You comin out or what?'

Gareth lets the options work their way through his mind. Might as well. PJ has gone quiet and it's Davodka now. Davodka is a French rapper with a brilliant line in social commentary and dystopian disaffection. He doesn't lecture and he doesn't use language gratuitously. He manages to marry a clinical diction with a pathetic wordplay. He really touches Gareth in an obtuse, asexual way. And he is also the fastest wordsmith Gareth has ever heard. He is brilliant when Gareth is cooking a stir-fry after sex over the kitchen table. But right now. Right now. He wants Ghostpoet. He wants Dial Tones. He wants the velvety, chocolate voice bemoaning the cruel reality of miscommunication between man and woman over a hip-hop melody. He doesn't know why he wants that. But he does. And the geez at number 23 doesn't seem to have discovered Ghostpoet yet. Maybe that's what Musicman needs right now. Maybe he's just had a bust-up with his girl, his woman, his yat, his bitch. Or whatever he calls her. Maybe he's gay.

Gareth gets up and looks across the road, mouthing to himself. It's Thursday. It is Thursday, isn't it? What's ee doin with rock n rap? On a Thursday? Gareth goes to the bathroom for a slash.

Chapter 5

The oak trees of Highcliffe Park always give off a comforting, sweet smell after an evening downpour. The feverous and the fetid of the early summer inferno have been cleansed, at least for now, and the daytime do-gooders are abed, bracing for another devil-red dawn. The insolence of busy-busy business is somnolent and the indolence of the ne'er-do-well is seeping from every lugubrious lair. The shivering leaf-life soothes the fractious wanderers, the twitchers and the psychotic pall-bearers who inhabit these hinterlands of urban decadence. And the black brushstroke of nightfall is occasionally flamed with the polka dot flashes of taxi-light, the hackneyed hackneys sucking in and spitting out the downtrodden and the drunk.

'Ta, mate. Keep the fuckin change, why don't yer.'

The tree-lined, meandering paths are tenebrous, cavernous, and ominous. Mafe can see Highcliffe Corner in the distance. To his left are the smell and the sound. But not the sight. He sees to the right but the right does not see him. And all the way from the library at one end to The Highcliffe Arms, on Highcliffe Corner, at the other, Shep noses his way through the maze of scents, never so far gone that Mafe cannot hear the sniff-sniff.

Seven letters in his head and The Board says RATION. Six empty spaces to the left is a triple word space and Mafe has sufficient letters to bridge and score heavily. He has four vowels in the seven-letter surplus and there IS a suffix to make the bridge. Damn. There was a time he'd have just seen it straight. Just like that. But Shep needs a piss and he's left The

Board half-done in The Optic. Mental Scrabble is a young man's game.

Still, he's quite glad to be out of there tonight. The Doc's wife is in and the Doc is vitriolic, evasive and charging full-whack for the ale. And Jonny says something to the Doc as he leaves. And he goes puce. Like he's just had his kidneys sucked out. Jonny is going now. Jonny is going to the library to revise. Jonny is proud to be announcing that he is going to the library. Jonny is proud to be declaring that he is going to revise. Jonny strides out, triumphant.

'Which library?'

Beany doesn't even look up from the hand-pull. 'Uni.'

'Howsi get in there?'

'I give 'im my pass. The bird in there never checks an' coseez weird she leaves 'im alone.'

The Doc grimaces. Like we all do, in agony, just before the hurt actually comes. Like sentient memory.

VITRIOLIC. Mafe has a V and an I and a T and an O in the surplus. VITRIORATION. On a triple word score. Must be 50+. One small problem. No such word. Mafe must have made up an entire language in his 35 years playing Scrabble against himself. The problem is the base word – RATION – six poxy points and it runs him into lexical culs de sac all over the board. Still, Jonny, bless 'im, is so happy to have helped his grandad put letters on the board, to be a part of Grandad's mysterious lexical world, that Mafe doesn't mind. It dries the tears in his eyes and sends him on his way with a smile. It's only six poxy points but be rational, Mafe tells himself, what price the happiness of your grandson? He harrumphs at his little *jeu de mots*. If he could just bridge, Mafe too would be smiling. And the thought of smiling brings a smile. Unwitting, subconscious, oedipal.

And it is at this point that she walks sharply by. All leather and chains and skulls and Doc Martens and exploding hair and purple and Death Metal and Nietzsche. Mafe loses the thread and Shep barks. Shep never barks. Mafe reins him in and stoops to calm him. There there. Just a student, anxious to get home.

A car pulls into the bus lay-by at Highcliffe Corner. The engine runs. But no one gets out.

And Mafe stays squat. He strokes Shep. He watches. He strokes. He watches. He strokes. She moves into eyeline and then away under the canopy. Lost her. He strokes. He watches. The car. YM06… can't see the rest… why would he need to… like the bridge on the Scrabble board… he needs closure. His mind is racing. A bead of sweat. No synergy – nature is soothing but the cerebral vortex swarms all over him.

And then it clicks.

'VITUPERATION. VITUPERATION. VITUPERATION. ON A TRIPLE WORD SCORE. 51.'

The car door clicks.

And as she opens it and stoops to kiss the lurching chauffeur full and heavy on the lips, she turns her head. And the car door light catches her creased brow and bright red lipstick. Snapshot.

'Excuse me?' She looks straight at him.

Mafe steps back into the shadow.

'Whatever.' And she gets into the car.

Mafe turns to walk back towards the library. And into an upright body. Point blank.

'Jonny. What are you doing here?'

Jonny stammers. Jonny stutters. Jonny spits at his words. Nothing.

'Are you ok, Jonny?'

Chapter 6

Europa Hymn is a layered, melodious, electronic soundscape punctuated by the bass-led, throbbing industrial machinery of Mr Martin Gore's gizmology. It is a beautiful, natural sea fret drifting inland for communion with the morning dew, only to disintegrate on the sharp, metallic edges of humanity and its eyesores. It is the struggle of humankind to find peace and emotional warmth in an angular, synthetic landscape. It is a paean to the human condition – at once the destroyer and the destroyed. It is musical masochism, wrapped in the irony that is cutting-edge technology being used to expose this galvanised dystopia. It is stripped back yet profound, austere yet all-consuming, brief yet enduring. It is brilliant. But most of the people who have heard it on Beany's speakers say it is shit. It is tuneless, aimless, pretentious crap and, in any case, where's the singin? These people only visit the once. Beany can't be doing with them. So he turns it up. And follows it with the whole album. Fuck 'em.

But this isn't coming out of Beany's speakers. This is coming from Musicman's window and it is obviously an extended remix. One reason to stay right where he is and roll another spliff. The other reason is that he needs to know what musical follow-up the strange geez across the road will go for. How will he choose to draw us from this dystopia? Personally, Beany would go for a Cure track called *The Catch*, a beautifully-strummed alleviation bemoaning a fleeting moment of lust. Love at first sight. Instant happiness snatched away by time and tide. But gorgeous, nevertheless. Or maybe an 8-minute tirade of seething, swarming guitar feedback by Mogwai – *You're Lionel Ritchie*, just to blast the melancholy out of the air. Or maybe something obtuse to arrest the mind, something lyrical to re-engage the wordsmith after this sonic invasion – how about Dylan's *Lily, Rosemary and the Jack of Hearts*, a dark tale of malevolence and misogyny in an American community, whose identity might still be easily recognised today?

And Beany finds it hard to extricate himself from his muse, to get a clear view on what he should do. And what he should say to Mum. The weed ain't helpin either. For sure, the obvious place to look for Jonny is the library and its environs. Jonny has no friends to speak of and he rarely leaves his room when he's not at school. So Mum is right, it is odd. Very odd.

But then Jonny has been uncharacteristically confident lately, albeit in short bursts. At times he puts on an air of purpose and single-mindedness which jars with the withdrawn, waspish personality Beany knows him to be. He has been oscillating wildly from cocksure student-pretender to delicate, shrinking schoolboy still desperate for his grandad's coat-tails. Beany supposes that he should have picked up on it and had a word. Not much he can do now, though.

The phone buzzes again.

MUM

ACCEPT OR DECLI

'Yes Mum, I'm on my way to the library to see if I can find him. It's shut now but maybe he's just takin a slow walk tonight. It's a nice night n all. I'll let you know.'

'It's bin pissin it down 'ere.'

Beany hesitates.

'Nice now, though. Best get goin. Let you know.'

And before she launches into another 'you need to take more care of your little brother he never had a dad to look over him yer know' lecture, he disengages and starts to lock down the digs for a quick getaway.

Beany cannot tolerate his mum when she starts to rake over the past and explain, for the gerzillionth time, how it was a tragedy for everyone when Dad went and that she wouldn't have made it through without Sean's boyish charm and cheer and joie de vivre and that Jonny has grown up without a father figure and he needs a male role model to give him an anchor and a direction. Not that Mum would use a term like 'joie de vivre'. One, because she wouldn't know it or what it means and, two, Mum's attitude to language is the same as her outlook on life – functional, unfussy, perfunctory, base.

Beany loves his mum and he forgives her all her foibles and idiosyncrasies but he has learned that he needs to detach to make his own way, to establish his own circle of friendship and enmity, love and loss, success and failure. It's not as if he hasn't sacrificed for them – he gave up a place at Queen's Cambridge to stay close to home.

Mum likes to think that he did it for Jonny but he actually did it for her. In many ways, Jonny is quite sorted and he can be very resilient when he needs to be – he has had to learn to be over years of mockery and sniping in the school corridors and on the park fields. But Mum, Mum is constantly lurching from one emotional crisis to another, looking for that absolute devotion and commitment from a man such that she might fill the huge hole left by Dad. Beany knows that she will never fill it. More like, she spends her life peering over the precipice and collapsing in a state of psychological vertigo when the latest bloke comes face to face with the chasm and runs a mile in the other direction.

The still evening air is suddenly filled with a saccharin, seductive west-coast drawl, delicately pondering what the sky was like when she was young. Beany is out the door and resolved to find his errant brother. And Musicman has just followed up Mr Gore's haunting of humanity with the so-called chill-out anthem *Little Fluffy Clouds*. The Orb made a business in the 80s and 90s out of bringing speeding, Vicks-sharpened students off the ceiling and onto a nice, cosy mattress, wrapping them in faux-childhood nostalgia and rocking them into a state of post MDMA karma. Rocking in the lullaby sense, of course, not with industrial quantities of guitar and a transvestite Freddie Mercury doing the hoovering. The music was, is, all soundscape, ambiance, harmony, melody and dazed, occasionally blippy Electronica. Undeniably, it is beautiful music but Beany needs to wake up and he is starting to worry now. Resilient, my arse. What are you thinking of, Beany? Jonny is a semi-functional, autistic, introverted misanthrope who snaps and snatches at perceived threats without the remotest notion of consequence and calamity. He could be half-conscious in a fuckin bush, for Christ's sake.

'Fuck. Fuck.'

Left his phone on the kitchen table. Beany turns and runs back to the house and the sexy, cathartic Californian voice only aggravates his sense of haplessness and anxiety. She says it was neat. This isn't. He picks up the phone and slams the door. And stops dead in his tracks.

'PJ Harvey? What the fuck. It's Thursday. Thursday is Electronica. This muppet's lost the plot.'

Barely half an hour later, Beany is back at his kitchen table. Mum called as he was halfway up the park road. Panic over. Jonny has just walked in. The lovely lad was walking his grandad home. Isn't he such a lovely boy? Said nothing about no library.

Beany draws on the spliff and turns to Gareth.

'Mum's 'ad a shag so that twat Saffi must be 'ome again. Yer can always tell. She's 'appy. Until the next round o' bruises… dunno what the fuck Jonny's up to, mind.'

Part 2
The Following Thursday

Chapter 7

'Fuck you, sir. I'm off to Behaviour.'

Dr Ramsbottom watches Karney push his books and assorted belongings onto the floor, grab his bag and walk for the door. 34 students are now watching Dr Ramsbottom minutely.

They are, of course, students. Not pupils. 'Pupils' implies diminution, subservience, inequality. At least, in the new Lexicon of Education it does. And we cannot have that. We cannot have teachers exercising any kind of moral, ethical, intellectual or, heaven forfend, physical authority over these fledglings of the utopian, inclusive democracy that is the modern school. Can we now? Our young people have rights, entitlements, a voice. And good old Karney has used his. And now he is voting with his feet. But as he is about to throw the door off its hinges, he stops, turns, strides directly at Dr Ramsbottom, uttering not a sound, and whips his mobile phone out of the teacher's hand.

'Think you'll find that's my property. Sir.'

'Behaviour' is just down the corridor. It is both a place and a concept. The place is open-all-hours to all students and yet, strangely, the three women who wield its conceptual sword are always 'busy' when a teacher goes to consult. The concept is equally elusive to the teachers.

The three witches, as they are known in the staff room, are not teachers. Never have been. They have never had to exact or extract anything productive from our young people. But they are experts. Unquestionably. Nobody is quite sure in what. But they very surely are.

'Behaviour' is a beehive of offices, a honeytrap of comfort-lounges, conceived and designed and run to give those disaffected by an education system which might just make academic demands on their delicate beings, a place of solace. Students who go there are counselled, humoured, entertained, amused, shown that being good to others is really rather easy – just let them do as they please. As long as they stay in school. That way, the badges of honour bestowed on this highly-regarded establishment for Inclusion and Attendance are renewed and Mrs Berry can sit proudly in front of the governors and declare a minimum of exclusions and certainly no expulsions. Not that that word exists anymore.

Just as the 'Library' is no longer in existence. As a concept it was far too aloof, intellectual, aspirational. Why would anyone want to go to a place where reading is the main purpose? Where education comes from pages not screens? Where there is no celebrity blogging and blagging his way through the minefield of modern pedagogical quandaries, such as is Raheem Sterling surplus to requirements at the 2018 World Cup or is Oli White actually called Oliver and should his YouTube videos be put on the National Curriculum… or what is left of it? So now we have a 'Learning Resource Centre'. And it is always quite amusing to see visitors to the school either looking hopelessly for the library or, better, licking the glass of the LRC and thinking, is that not a library?

Dr Derek Ramsbottom is in his twenty-eighth year of teaching. His previous career as an export assistant ended when the big mouth of US business swallowed his great grandad's engineering company and decided that neither his experience nor his training nor his expertise nor, come to that, his surname, were on the menu. His £2,000 pay-off freed up his table for a new, shiny, dynamic, malleable, hungry executive. The execution of this executive was swift, silent, unflinching.

So here he is, infusing and enthusing a new generation of linguists, opening their horizons to a world of imagery and pathos, omniscient narrators and onomatopoeia.

Except that, at this precise moment, he is helpless.

It is not that his authority is being called into question – he had none anyway. Behaviour and Behaviour alone has taken ownership of that – the authority, that is, to reach out to the student, to ask him his point of view, to empathise and sympathise with the petty injustices of the disorganised and disengaging teacher, to question the teacher's account and his actions in the face of 'minor' infringements, infringements such as the systematic and wilful disruption of an entire lesson.

It is not that he has failed to dispatch his duties – he has called the register and started his lesson with a clear objective. But Karney is quite within his 'rights' to come and go as he pleases. He has a 'red-card', allowing him to check in and out of lessons as he sees fit, as and when he needs to take stock, keep his counsel, calm down.

It is not that he doesn't have a plan for the lesson or a love for his subject.

It is just that, when one or two students don't give a shit, the momentum carried by the able and the assiduous wins out. But when eight or nine students are openly ignorant and oblivious, it doesn't. And this is Bottom Set. They know that, in two months, they will be asked to make choices. But none will involve English Literature. So who gives a fuck? Not Karney, or Cameron, or Tom or Ben or Reece or Daniel or Marielle or Shanyka.

And after twenty-seven years, in truth, neither does Derek Ramsbottom. The vocation of yonder year has long since become an exercise in self-survival, babysitting, cajoling, coercing, placating. So they draw mind-maps, storyboards and tourist brochures. If this were Art it would be dot-to-dot, colour by numbers, stencil-shapes.

'Is ee gonna be kicked out for that, sir?'

'Of course not, James. I'll have a chat with him later. He's obviously upset so it's right that he go and calm down. I'm sure he didn't really mean what he said.'

'Ee fuckin did.'

'Excuse me, Selica?'

'Nuffin, sir. Dint say owt.'

Chapter 8

'Mornin dude.'

'Easy.'

The slurp of flip-flops on lino. The nasal clearance, guttural, all lion re-establishing his territory. Kettle on.

'You 'avin one?'

'Yeah, gon then.'

'Fuck me, I couldn't get off at all last night. Musta bin 4 by the time I went out.'

Beany laughs. Gareth stands in the lounge doorway.

'What you fuckin laughin at?'

'You, man. You're a dick.'

'N you're not?'

Beany does his Gareth impression – creases his brow, left hand cruises through his dark, tidal, uncoiffed hair, arches his back to invite the semi-clad lady on to him. The voice is caricature camp. Beany sounds like he's about to start singing *When I'm Cleaning Windows*.

'I just don't get it. I go to bed at 11 with my cafetière, read for a while to make my eyes tired…n I just can't get off. I just don't understand.'

Gareth isn't camp. His voice is gravelly and his torso is long but broad and slightly rugger-bugger hench, Neanderthal. And Beany is anything but dark. He would be ginger but the locks have already been arrested by the ginger police. Which, of course, is what makes the impression all the more ridiculous and funny. It is also flecked with a northern flatness. Although Beany tries very hard to disguise it.

'Fuck off. If anyone's gay round 'ere, it's you, yer back-scuttler.'

'50p in the beer pot, dick'ed. Non-PC language on a weekend.'

'Fuck off. It ain't the weekend n your shitty impression of me wasn't then?'

'No.' Obsequious, posh voice. 'I think you'll find my language was entirely within the regulations, dear boy. The tone was insinuative but the diction was all above board.'

'You called me gay, you hairy-arsed lezzer.'

'Oh, that be another 50 then. In fact, it's a quid – hairy-arsed and lezzer counts as two offences.'

'Ah, fucksake.'

The kettle clicks. Gareth shuffles off.

Gareth Simpson is reading Food Science. Not the one with the aprons and the oven-gloves and the Heston Bloomin'eck affectations. Not the one through which Nigella has probably pouted and preened. The proper one. The one with Chemistry and Biology and Mathematics in it. The one with big thick books to read. Books with no pictures. And constant references to big thick glossaries. The ones in which the maths is all letters mixed with numbers and Sodium Chloride and Monosodium Glutamate are never referred to by their common names. He's so good at it that the geeks have asked him to stay on and do a doctorate. And he drinks a full cafetière before bed and then wonders why he can't sleep. He could probably write out the equation explaining the stimulus effect of the cocoa bean on the human brain. But it doesn't stop him doing it time and again.

Gareth Simpson left school at 17. No one invited him to do it. No one knew he was going to do it. He just woke up one day, packed a rucksack and left. The school left a message on his mum's answerphone but she was often away and by the time she'd picked it up he was in Le Vigan, shagging a French bird under canvas. Mum was so relieved when he came up for air that she paid off the school fees, told them he was leaving and sent him some money to keep him easy for a few months. On the promise that he came back for her birthday. Mum never flinched at bailing him out – Dad died when he was 9 and she felt so guilty that she put much of the inheritance into Gareth's well-being. Or rather, her own – it made her feel better to lavish him. But her son spent most of it on weed and whizz and the hallowed old school, which was so posh that the lacrosse sticks had to be carbon if you wanted to play First Team, took a rather dim view of his wasteful and ungentlemanly behaviour. They'd have kicked him out soon enough anyway if he hadn't walked.

Le Vigan is a beautiful little town in the Cévennes, buried under the Mont Aigoual in the no man's land between the Pyrenees and the Mediterranean coast. It does tourism very well. And the wi-fi reception is rubbish. So Gareth played druggy and dandy for a while into the long, balmy evenings. And then got bored one day. As often seemed to happen with him, the girl started to take it a bit too seriously – specifically, she turned up at his foxhole two nights on the trot. So he packed up the next morning and headed for Montpellier on a bus. That's when Mum got hold of him and he agreed to do a correspondence A Level course when he got back if she'd let him stay out there for the summer. He didn't really want to go home but Mum was alone and lonely and sometimes the guilt jarred him to the bone. Mainly when he'd done one too many tabs.

The course was a doddle. He worked the bars, did a bit of pizza delivery, hooked up with his old supplier and rattled off a few modules and essays and mini research papers. His tutor was impressed and the A grades came rather nicely. As did a university place.

He met Sean at a house party in his first year and Beany loved him. In fact, it was Gareth who first called him Beany because his flat South Yorkshire vowels were pure Sean Bean. Gareth's mates would give him a quid to do his impression when they were all hammered. It was shite but Beany loved the attention and it cemented the slightly dangerous friendship he'd long wanted. For Beany, Gareth was the Mediterranean player. His was the rich, dark hair. His was the mellifluous, slightly melancholic voice. His was the easy athleticism and the beautiful wardrobe. His was the freedom of a life untethered by parochialism and family dependency. And for Gareth, Beany was pure *Coronation Street* – all eeebygum n fish n chips n beef n gravy n ginnels n cobbled shitters n Mum and Bro n Our Lass just rount corner n owt n nowt. Yorkshire, Yorkshire, born n bred, thick in th'arm n thick in th'ead. He was safe, he was the boy Gareth never had next door. He was a lighthouse on Gareth's heavy seas.

And he is always there. Always.

Gareth shuffles back in.

'Oh, and don't you dare wear that fuckin Mr Blobby suit for your interview today.'

'You remembered! How lovely of you, Mr Simpson. There is a heart in there after all.'

'Don't be gay.'

'Another 50 in the pot. Oh and I might just wear that lovely MnS number anyway. Just for you.'

'Look, fuck face. You won't get outta this house with that fat suit on, you tit. You wouldn't get a job in a fuckin Macky Ds wearing that thing.'

'All the more reason to wear it. Don't want the damn job anyway.'

'You need it man. It's cash for your PhD and it's perfect experience in preparation for your life as a hotshot, twatty lawyer.'

'Aye, well, I'm fast goin off that shitty idea.'

'You're a dick. Right, get some toast on, I'm going to dig out that sharp blue number for your interview.'

Gareth shuffles off up the stairs. Again.

Beany shouts up after him.

'I won't wear the fuckin thing, dick. N you still ain't cleaned the grill so the toast ain't hapnin.'

Gareth leans round the banister.

'I'm off for a shit before you get in here preening.'

Chapter 9

Hunched like a grovelling shakespearian witch over the alphabet soup, she prods and pokes at the keys. She is dropping numbers into the cauldron; very deliberately, very painstakingly. Glaring through the glare to see if the concoction is just right. It is. Of course it is. Must be a few score papers already this year. Easy does it. No trace. No handwriting anymore. Just tap tap tap, ping. Next question.

No one is coming to nosy. The sign on the door says no to the wanderers and the wonderers. As if anyone is wandering or wondering. Those who aren't stirring their own pot have long since gone back to their sanctuary of selective cognition. And they know. They all know. Compliance and complicity are easy bedfellows. Just a letter or two, here and there, on someone's script, draws one from the other. Not nosy anymore. Just cosy. Snug in the sheets of silence. Wrapped. Trapped.

Except.

Except that Dr Ramsbottom is looking through the glass in the door. Not nosy. Not wondering. No need. It's blindingly obvious. Two computers and two staff. No students. But it's ok. No handwriting anymore. No trace.

Trouble is. The exam is live. It's online. Now. And this is the Examination Room. And he has been informed by the Exams' Officer that Jonny Hainsworth is doing an exam. But Jonny Hainsworth is not in the room. Oh no, Dr Ramsbottom cannot see right into the corners of the room. Because of its shape. Because of the shady light. Because of the way Wilhelm and her lackey have arranged the furniture. But he knows Jonny

Hainsworth is not in the room. He is definitely not in the room. He knows because Jonny Hainsworth is with *him*, in *his* room, re-drafting an essay on *Touching The Void* by Joe Simpson. Something Dr Ramsbottom feels like he's doing every day.

But it's ok. He is outside. He remains outside. He cannot go in. Examination rules. And he knows nothing.

He should, he supposes, go and inform the Examinations' Officer about the 'apparent oversight'. But he doesn't. It wouldn't be worth it. It wouldn't be news to her. She's known for a long time. Compliant. Complicit. Like everyone else in this hallowed establishment. And, in any case, the duty of the Examinations' Officer would be to report it to, well, the Senior Leadership Team and, in this case, Ms Wilhelm. And Ms Wilhelm is in the Examination Room. With, or without, Jonny Hainsworth.

Dr Ramsbottom wanders back to his room, the word *omertà* bouncing around his conscience. He heard it used on Oprah Winfrey a while ago and it cropped up in Mafe's evening serenade with the Scrabble board shortly after. He looked it up. 'A code of silence about criminal activity and a refusal to give evidence to the police.' Its origins are in Italian dialect and Lance Armstrong had claimed it to be at the heart of the Tour de France peloton, for which reason he had decided to, quote 'get with the program' in his days as a professional cyclist.

And, most interestingly to this Doctor of the English language and inveterate wordsmith, it is a variant of the word *umiltà*, which means humility. In the exclusive peloton that is the Senior Leadership Team, there may well be *omertà*, he thinks, but there is certainly no *umiltà* whatever.

Maybe Dr Ramsbottom just needs to get with the program.

Chapter 10

Mafe is reading. Mafe is always reading. Well, when he isn't playing with his words or walking his dog.

Mid-afternoon is the perfect time in the Optic. The air is still, the musty mélange of ageing upholstery, leftovers and hops gives it a homely, Sunday-afternoon smell. It's like breathing the inside of an old beer barrel or flicking the pages of an antique book in the Bodleian Library.

The occasional noise of clinking glass, shuffling newspaper and vibrating phone keeps the world distant, but there if he needs it. A misanthrope's perfect night out – presence without the people, warmth without the mealy-mouthed, windy words.

Perfect for reading.

Mafe is in a café in a surreal French town, opposite the Divorce Courts. Separating couples tend to kill time in this café with their lawyers, staring and glaring at one another before the final act is done. And, of course, in a lovely twist of fate, it is where some of these couples realise, senses sharpened by the imminence of closure and the rich aniseed of the Ricard, that they love one another. A good number walk out, hand in hand, leaving their lawyers vexed and perplexed.

Mafe loves the childish simplicity of Eric Orsenna's ideas, his easy description of a people trying to make sense of the world around it. Trying to make sense where there is none. And, in a state of optimism, naivety or desperation – or a combination – seeking out what is important.

And, lovelier still, Mafe reads in the original language, missing none of the nuance and the pathos so often lost in translation.

And as he pauses to watch Nails polish the bar, the cloth occasionally squeaking over the pumps and the puffpuff of the cleaning stuff punctuating the quietude, Mafe reflects on the wonderful gift his teachers gave him all those years ago.

Mafe was born in Bradford to Yorkshire mill folk. His parents spoke fluent Yorkshire and could understand a smattering of Lancashire. Anything north of the Ouse or south of the Don and Dad was knackered, resorting to loud gesticulation and louder language to get what he wanted. Grandma grew up a seamstress in a mill-house and barely spoke Bradford, that being best part of ten miles from Saltaire. So it came as a bit of an uncomfortable surprise when Mafe wandered casually through O Levels and A Levels in two European languages and ended up at university doing a degree in both. By that time Dad was adamant that even French wine had gone down the pan and that New World wines would ensure the belittling of a nation which had stabbed us in the back after we'd bailed it out in the Second World War.

And decades later, France and England are still trying to work out the love-hate relationship endemic in business and pleasure. How it is that we are so close and yet so very different? Why do we do so much trade with and go on so many holidays so frequently to a country whose outlook and attitude we abhor? Do we want them to be more like us? Do we want to be more like them? *Vive la différence*. And who are 'they' anyway?

Mafe gets excited about very little these days. But the homogenisation of the social, cultural and creative world to facilitate big business is one red rag to his polyglot bull. So he voted out. No thanks to a European Union of mono-commercialism, mono-culturalism and monotonous mono-lingualism. Don't call him a racist, a xenophobe, a little-Englander. Don't patronise him with your glib, ignorant, urbanised liberal fascism. Don't tell him he's wrong and you're right. You with your polka dot catchphrases and your pinstripe strategy and your comprehensive portfolios and your crass commuter critique of all those traditionalists who have long since retreated to civilisation and common sense.

He speaks three languages. He reads foreign literature. His grandson listens to French rap. And he enjoys French food and applauds French national pride and he delights in their fight against Americanisation. Like Morrissey said – or so Jonny tells him – America's head is as big as its belly; and that's too big. France has a National Academy for the protection of its own language, for goodness sake. How wonderfully anachronistic is that?

And Erik Orsenna sits on it. In the chair formerly occupied by Louis Pasteur, the man who tackled rabies with a microscope and went on to become the best milk monitor of all time.

'Saw Jonny wandering the park the other night, Nails. Bit concerned about him really. A lad like that shouldn't be out in a place like that on his own at that time.'

'What was ee doin?' Nails is mid-stroke on the guest ales.

'I really don't know. It must have been after closing time here. I was walking the dog up near Highcliffe Corner and I turned to head back towards the library end and he just appeared.'

Mafe is pulling at his woollen sleeves, as though the Scrabble has just paid a healthy dividend.

'He seemed very uncomfortable when he saw me and he was wide-eyed, like he'd taken a lick of MDMA or some such.'

He hooks his thumb into the little hole worn into the jumper.

'Don't know what to make of it really.'

'Yeah. Sean's been worried about him too. Think things ain't so good at home with Mum. N that boyfriend seems like a real bastard.'

'Mmm. He's been coming and going in and out of Jonny's life for a while, so I hear, and it is totally unsettling him. I think Sean has tried to reason with her but she's not listening.

Meantime Jonny has just withdrawn into his music and his autism. And he's got re-sits coming up. Heaven knows, Nails, what do we do?'

Nails has dropped the cloth and come over to Curmudgeon Corner. Tall, faux-blond, all lips, tits n bum. In between, a butcher's dog wouldn't have much to snaffle after a couple of small steaks, as Mafe's wife might have said. Slender but untoned.

It had taken Mafe a good while to work out how the Doc and Nails clicked. But, looking back, he doesn't know why it took so long – she is anathema to the politically-correct, worthy teachers surrounding and smothering the Doc during the day. The bawdy, careless humour, the hedonistic disregard for the morning after and the voluptuous manipulation of manhood is a potent mix and, in his occasional moments of sexual lucidity, Mafe sees exactly what drew him.

'Dunno, chuck. Eez one o those blokes who people will always take advantage of cos he's so naïve an kind. Sean needs to look out for 'im, that's for sure.'

'Mmm. Tell you what. He really needs to get through these exams and move onto a college course in which he can use his cognitive and memory skills. People think he's slow but, tell you what, you explain logic and process to him properly and he really gets it. And he has a real memory for the detail, Nails. He's just not particularly erudite and he simply cannot relate to the people around him. He'd be great in a lab, polishing and adjusting microscopes, calibrating scales and categorising test tubes.'

'Who would?'

Derek almost brings the door and the weather with him. If his entrance through the side door had been a ball into a net, John Motson might have used the word 'pile-driver'. Angry, Derek doesn't even wait for an answer as Mafe and Nails look at one another, nervous, as though they've been caught in flagrante.

'That place is gonna be the fuckin death o me. I'm the only bloody one with keys to that cupboard n I've bin keepin coursework in there for 12 years. No one would dare go in there, let alone tamper with the coursework. I put some fuckin GCSE coursework in there 2 months ago, alphabetically ordered, all marked and annotated with cover sheets ready for despatch to the Board. I noted all the provisional grades down in my mark-book. Job done.'

He stands in the middle of the pub, tatty old cricket bag still swinging around his shoulders.

'I go in there today to find 8 scripts have been moved and brought to the top and when I check the cover sheets, the marks are not the ones I have on the system. And then when I look more closely, the work is not the same as the original essays.'

Derek Ramsbottom – Dr Derek Ramsbottom – is leaning on the Stella pump.

The Doc likes to lean: lean on the solid oak bar as he passes the time with the locals; lean on the rusty old coolers as he takes another verbal tirade from the missus; lean on the myriad books in his study as he searches his encyclopaedic lexicon for yet another word to keep Mafe happy; lean on the steering wheel as Ellie pleasures his manhood. Lean on the system. Lean on his colleagues. Lean on memory and experience and guile to convince the bigwigs that he can still produce the silk purse from the sow's ear. Lean on his reputation.

The Doc exists. And he is happy. Just to exist. It is some years since he invested. Really invested. In his life, his family, his friends, his job, his appearance, his body, his mind.

By day, he mollycoddles an assortment of social and intellectual stereotypes and spare parts through the usual array of flawed literary concoctions. The brains and the brawn, the dull and the dim, the mumblers and the misfits, the waifs and the strays, the ripe and the ribald, they all pass through. And these days, he notices fewer and fewer – the wise and the witty, the vile and the violent all come to mind. But they are few. And diminishing. They are all bored. Bored with the tired, old curriculum, bored with the mealy-mouthed mumbo-jumbo, bored with the levels and the targets and the tests and the fresh starts and the insidious and unrepentant coercion, bored with the curmudgeons and the cunts in front of them.

The Doc used to be the pied-piper of Highcliffe, trumpeting the lyrical loud mouthery and loucherie of the Bard, the fey and the feigning of Brontë and Austen and Lawrence, the mellifluous and the mundane of Coleridge and Keats, the clever and the coruscating of Larkin and Hughes. But these days, he's like a misguided pedagogical tourist, wandering down the autumnal promenade in a cerebral maelstrom, students passing him in all directions. Some are meaningful, purposeful, ruddy in their stridency; others loaf by, distracted by empty bottles, the tic-tac of tat all around and the graffiti. And all the while the swell and the sea-spit of tidal behaviour batter the front, debilitating, demoralising, damning. In short, he's one of the curmudgeonly. And he is, without doubt, a cunt.

Some people get to the other end of the seafront and sit in the shade, remembering the sunshine and the buckets and spades and the sandcastles so beautifully pawed. The Doc doesn't. For the last five years – or maybe more – it's like he's been watching the tsunami approaching from afar. It's only a matter of time before he is swept up and drowned. It will be quick, of that he has no doubt. It would just be nice if it took the whole bloody system with it. Yes, that is what the system needs. It needs deep-cleaning with saltwater. It needs razing to the ground. And among the drowned may be good colleagues and friends and wits and waterhole comrades. The odd one is even a local at the Optic. But backwashed into oblivion will hopefully be the sly and the sycophantic, the apologists and the actors, the twats and the cheats.

By night, he inebriates and infects the muddled minds of the forever middle-aged and the failed middle-classes in a dingy old student boozer. The casual and the cantankerous of his ranting is punctuated with the long-winded damnation of our realities and the meandering nonsense of the universal and unilateral resolutions, spat out in diatribe and almost instantly forgotten. Everybody and nobody is to blame.

The Optic is like a spider's web. Mostly it is still, near-silent, a gossamer distillation of a half-hung humanity. These people are the remnants, the clingers-on, the dregs of the system. Occasionally, there is a scurry of savagery – the 'I tell you what I fuckin thinks' and the 'what thi should a dun wos' and the 'for fucksakes' are suddenly thirsty and the nod goes out to the Doc. Same again. Same old.

In this pub, tomorrow *does* come. Tomorrow is real, tangible, predictable. Because tomorrow is today. It's just the same.

And ironically, that is how the Doc wants it. The man who wants to escape the crushing collateral of the daily is never happier than when he is staring through the pumps at the browbeaten yet volcanic facades of those who live his reality, who will get up and go to work in the morning until they are told not to and who say yes to the requests to which they should say no and no to the questions to which they should say yes.

Mafe goes back to playing with his sleeve.

'For fucksake. Someone has re-written entire pieces of coursework, re-marked them and, waddaya know, it's all gone from D to B and even A in some cases. The level of cheatin in that bloody place 'as got ridiculous. Fuckin ridiculous. I'm fuckin goin straight into Berry's office tomorrow and she gives me a plausible explanation or she gets my resignation.'

At this point Nails would, once upon a time, slink up to him, press her chest against his chin and invite a little conjugal amnesia. But the outbursts are happening weekly these days and, frankly, the Doc looks pretty shit with his clothes off – it's all belly n bluster n no oomph. And, in any case, she's heard that threat a hundred times and the Doc is about as likely to carry it through as he is to tell her he loves her.

'Just let it go, man. Why do you care?'

Wrong thing to say.

'Fuckin Jesus. Not you n all. I might av bin in this game a bloody long time n I don't give a shit about the twats upstairs anymore but these kids are being completely manipulated n it's not right on any level.'

'Get him a pint, Nails. Did I see the IPA lorry pull in earlier? A few of those'll sort the old boy out.'

Mafe really doesn't like it when the Doc is like this. Not because he cares about the Doc, although he does, not because he cares about the principle here, although he does, but because it conjures images of him clearing his desk not so very long ago, taking blue-tac and old photos off the wall he'd worked under for over 20 years, reducing his professional contribution to a few scraps in a hastily-cobbled brown box, gently hugging his secretary goodbye and being led from the building like a paedophile, bowed by the two security guards escorting him out whilst removing his I.D. card and his laptop paraphernalia.

Early bath. Fishing leave. Shelved. No good to anyone anymore. Not the man for the job. Need fresh blood, a fresh outlook, clarity of vision, embrace the change, sweep away the dead wood… blah blah fuckin blah.

'Mafe, don't you gerrit, you stupid old git? Your bloody grandson is at that school and guess where he sits in the pantheon of academic greatness? Yes, you guessed it, right on the C/D borderline. Precisely one of those students the fuckin witch Wilhelm is 'helping', Mafe. The corruption which pushed you out the door only a few years ago is now being perpetrated on your grandson. And do you think for one minute that the witch is being open and transparent with little Jonny when she is helping him? No, of course fuckin not. Is that what you want, Mafe? Your grandson being a willing accessory to the cheating that has undermined the entire education system and lost you your livelihood? What the fuck? My fuckin God.'

Mafe stares. Glazed. He is not in the moment. He is in his head. And although he is conscious of the need to respond to the Doc's onslaught, he is not hearing the Fs and the Bs and the Cs but the dullards and the disingenuous wishing him well, thanking him for his years of service, recounting tales of derring-do on trips and close-shaves in the classroom, for which someone in the office would no doubt be reprimanding him these days.

Nails defaults and brings him a pint of No3.

He watches it settle. He watches the Doc settle. The cloud lifts to the surface and dissipates, almost, leaving a moment of golden radiance before he brings the glass to his lips and takes a long, thirsty draw. The moment of clarity is fleeting but all the more beautiful for it.

'Sorry, Mafe. I'm very sorry. You don't deserve that. I'm sorry. That one's on the house.'

'Cheers.'

'Cheers, old boy.'

The Doc retires to his study via the bar and goes to get a strong coffee. Once upon a time he'd sit at the bar and mark books with his first pint of the evening. But he's long ago given that up. He started getting a red nose and anxiety attacks in the morning.

So the marking had to go.

Peer assessment is a fabulous ruse. Utterly without pedagogical merit as the kids flick and tick page after page, error after error, with impunity and inaccuracy. And hand the work back to their mates, with a nudge-nudge, wink-wink. Work marked, kids are happy, the Doc has no marking and he just puts any old mark down in his book as they call them out to him. Who cares? No one ever refers to mark-books anymore because they prove that there is indeed an intellectual hierarchy, a pecking order, and that we are not all the same, that we cannot all achieve the same level. But in the modern system, everyone has to be above-average. So mark-books are not of interest to the Senior Leadership Team.

'You talk to Sean about Jonny, D?'

The Doc has come back into the bar looking for his bag. He leans over the bar holding a mug. The World's Greatest Teacher. He never did tell Nails who bought that for him. Or the signed copy of a Carol Ann Duffy anthology with an unnerving number of kisses on the inside cover.

'On and off, yeah. He's a strange one, isn't he? Apparently he's started getting a little fetish for a student in the University library. Ellie, she's called. Jonny seems to think she has taken his phone number.'

'Mmm, that's funny cos I saw him the other night, walking towards Highcliffe Corner from the library end of the park. It was well after closing time and I was asking Nails about it. It's all a bit worrying, especially given his unsettled home life. I do worry about that boy. I'm not sure Sean realises how vulnerable he is and, of course, he is wrapped up in student life and all that comes with it.'

Mafe wipes the froth from his top lip.

'Bloody hell. Bloody hell.'

'What? Don't tell me the No3 is off again, old boy?'

Three things annoy Nails. One is the Doc. But a bad pint and wishy-washy fish n chips are worse. Much worse. This is Yorkshire. We serve proper pints and proper fish n chips n if either is bad, then Yorkshire needs to sort itself the fuck out. This ain't London. We don't do a fuckin marketin campaign n send a young twat out on commission to expand portfolios n grow customer retention rates. We sort the fuckin barrel out, gerron tut brewer n give im a pastin. Old school.

'No, no, Nails. It's fine. It's such a lovely pint. Thanks. But it just occurred to me – just before I saw Jonny the other night, I was passed by a young lass, student in all likelihood, approaching Highcliffe Corner. All in black, leathers, Dr. Martens, sulky, you know the type. Well, just as she neared the bus stop, a car pulled up, Picasso it was, just like your model, D. She got in, I think. Anyway, as she opened the car door, I turned to go back the other way and that's when I bumped into Jonny. Quite literally, as a matter of fact. He was right behind me.'

Nails turns to the bar to look for a reaction. The Doc blows out his cheeks to avoid spitting coffee over the newly-polished bar.

'And the strangest thing of all is that Jonny was very shy and evasive about the whole thing. He uttered a few words, which I really didn't hear because of the passing cars, and then pretty much ran off across the road to Highcliffe Moor. I presume he went home but it's most unlike him not to give me the time of day. He'll always come and talk to me, will Jonny. I don't really understand it.'

The Doc swallows the coffee. Hard. Mafe looks straight into Nails' eyes. Fortunately for the Doc, she's still seething at the thought of a bad pint and soggy fish batter. She's oblivious to the Doc's flush discomfort. He'd make a terrible poker player.

But Mafe sees what he thought he might see.

That night, as he walked home pondering Jonny's uncharacteristic haste, it occurred to him that if Jonny was following that girl, then he would have remembered the number plate on the car, particularly had he done this before. So, over a lull in the Scrabble the other day, he'd just dropped in the question about having a photographic memory, comforting Jonny in his moment of need as he exuded nervousness about his exams.

'For example, Jonny, I can never remember number plates of cars I have had, or telephone numbers of old friends. But Grandma used to remember them all, just like that. Isn't that amazing? You've obviously inherited your Grandma's extraordinary memory.'

'Maybe, Grandad. I know Mum's number plate, and Saffi's is DL04 TYN and I've only seen that one a couple of times cos he's just got a new one.'

'Ok. Here's a test for you then. When I saw you the other night, late in the park, there was a car waiting in the bus stop and a girl went to get into it. Do you remember that one?'

'YMO7 KTU.' Jonny had barely allowed Mafe to finish his question.

Thought so, thought Mafe.

Mafe doesn't have to go outside the pub to check the Picasso in the spot marked 'Landlord'. And just at that minute, as Nails gets up to go and check the cellar, Mafe catches the Doc's eye. It might as well be emblazoned on his forehead – YMO7 KTU.

Chapter 11

Beany is scribbling in his diary. The bus jolts and jerks up the hill from town and he struggles to keep the writing legible. It isn't neat at the best of times.

Beany is uncomfortable. He hates wearing suits and the fashion for slim-fit irritates. He spends the day thinking he's clipped, ripped or unknowingly unzipped it and he feels like he is exposing himself in some way. He feels like a wanker. Gareth The Player wouldn't let him go to the interview in his old school number. Beany loves the commodious, double-breasted MnS get-up. Well, as much as he's ever going to love a suit. But Gareth would fight him as let him walk out in that. And Gareth is too beautiful to fight.

'You're a bloody linguist not a friggin second-hand car salesman, for fucksake. Do you want the job or not, knucklehead?'

Of course, Beany doesn't want the job. He doesn't want the job at all. He wants to carry on living the life he lives now – lounging for Great Britain's Olympic Lounging Team, reading his weight in musty old books bought from Oxfam every week, drinking and smoking himself slowly into oblivion and keeping a close eye on his bro and mo. Oh and expanding his music collection to fill the entire back wall of his lovely, spacious, airy student room. Other than that, Beany has two aims in life: one, to rid his family of the hideous Saffi, Mum's boomerang boyfriend, who keeps coming back no matter how far he is cast adrift; two, to find a girl who will love him for the kind, perceptive but rather parochial man that he is becoming. And not expect too much of him in bed. Because Beany finds the whole sex thing overwhelming. He is ginger, he is balding, he is not endowed with even a modicum of athletic prowess and neither is he endowed for great sexual exploits. He knows he has disappointed in the past and for a good while now he has retreated to the world of cerebral, conscious abstinence, hoping to be afforded a hint of respect for his elective timidity or, better, sought after by a beautiful Goth who finds his reticence alluring.

Riding back now, bouncing up and down on the bus, he is confident that a choice between ribboned portfolios and ribbed penis-protectors is not imminent. The interview was a disaster in which he lost argument after argument and cited irrelevant precedents in defence of indefensible jurisdiction. His friends and family might think him a linguist. But, as yet, not a single linguist has been persuaded.

The bus stops again. People wave bits of laminated card at the driver, utter inanities at the driver with little reciprocation beyond a harrumph, most-humbly apologise to the driver for deigning to travel without the right change, swear at the fuckin driver for not allowing them to travel with insufficient change and get thrown off, and ask the driver when the next bus to so-and-so is due, to which his answer can be guessed with little intuition. Safe to say it includes the word off. They are lucky he allows them to launch themselves back off the vehicle before engaging first gear again.

The usual array of passengers is dotted about the seats: warty old natterers with even older shopping trolleys, talking about the days when a loaf was three pence ha'penny and milk tasted of cows' arses; vaguely menacing middle-aged men who could be misanthropic dons of great cerebral import or social outcasts on a Register or two; call-centre dollies squeezed into River Island's entire summer collection, chewing and spitting gum and gossip and forever devolving and denying responsibility for anything, with endless he-saids n she-saids; and the occasional bourgeois lady, dressed like an ostentatious wedding cake just to go n get a few things and whose face is

65

disgusted with everything and everyone. She shouldn't be on the bus. It is clearly beneath her. There is a permanent smell of shit on the end of her snout and most people she has ever met or will ever meet wish the bus were on top of her rather than beneath her.

And Beany wonders why the simple bus, a handy, communal provision which is a lifeline to thousands, has such power to make even the most prosperous and cheerful people seem lonely, sad and miserable.

Grandad won't travel on them. He has no car and hasn't driven for years in any case. Just as well – he'd be as much a physical liability and nuisance on the road as he is a verbal one in pretty much any public space. Particularly The Optic. The punters don't realise how thankful they should be to the creator of Scrabble. It shuts him up. For hours. As for the bus, he'd rather go without or walk, he says. Bloody piss-infested hearses clogging up the road to the cemetery, he says. It always makes Beany laugh. He suspects Granny came up with the phrase. As is so often the case with biddies, Mafe spent many a moment berating his wife's generalisations, bigotry, casual racism and overbearing intolerance; only to quote her at will after her death with both humour and rueful nostalgia.

Beany goes back to his diary.

I see through you.
You with your polka dot catchphrases
And your pinstripe strategy
And your comprehensive portfolios.

And you see through me.
Me with my yawning mornings
And my giro drinking
And my indolent indifference.

But you see nothing, Mr Man,
But a pale imitation of your own ego.
Cliché. Touché.

You're boring, Mr Man.
You're so fucking boring.

Beany closes his diary. The bus is moving again and his stop is coming up. He's about to ring the bell but someone on the top deck gets there first. He stands, swinging his man bag over his head and moves towards the front of the bus, swaying with the vehicle's movement as it jerks into top gear. Only for the driver to start slowing and revving down the gearbox ready for a stop. The girl who rang the bell comes tottering down the stairs. Tight, short, black dress, white heels, fancy handbag. Pudding legs and pudding face, orange bottle tan and pouting like a cosmetic-counter tart. Vaguely ugly but nice tits. Beany ushers her down the last step to stand in front of him. No real motive behind it, except perhaps some distant chivalrous instinct. But it gives him chance to have a look at the backside. Flabby. Unexercised. Limp. And the dress is hiding very little. The scent is almost overpowering. It's a cheap splash of nondescript chemicals masquerading as the fermentations of an entire fresh Mediterranean pasture and the fancy bottle probably cost more to make than the contents. You could say style over substance but this lass certainly doesn't lack corporal substance. There's a lot of her. Beany reckons about six pints and he'd have a second look. Still, for some reason he doesn't really fathom, he's quite disappointed when she clomps off the bus and straight into some gym-bunny's biceps and pectorals.

He walks down St Christopher Road and turns up Titus Terrace. He won't be doing this much longer.

The door is ajar. Beany steps straight into the kitchen for a brew.

'Ok, Beany? Get it?'

'They're calling me. Not holding my breath. He was a twat.'

'A twat with a nice car n a fit wife.'

'A twat's a twat. N he was camp as tits. No wife there, mate. Put kettle on... what you gonna do, anyway? You ain't even got a suit.'

'Fair point. Least you makin an effort. Stepdad called again. Mithering. Told him I'd sent in a few apps. Dunno, travel probably.'

'What with?'

'Deposit for this place, when we gerrit back.'

'Oh aye. As if Spencer's giving us shit. 'Ave you seen the state of the cooker? That's yer 800 quid alone. And you still owe me for the Rentakil geez.'

'I wasn't even here, man.'

'Yeah but they were your cans behind the tele.'

'Bullshit. They were mostly Boddies n I don't even drink that piss.'

'Jesus, half of 'em were Stella and you're the only one who drinks wife beater. Anyway, all for one and one for all. You weren't gonna be able to watch tele with a friggin wasps' nest fussin round a bunch of half-empty beer cans stuffed down the back of the screen, now were you?'

'Fair do's.'

Chapter 12

There is noise in the kitchen again.

Jonny puts on his headphones but the screams pierce the screech of the guitar, the angry bass of the male voice vibrates through the floorboards and resonates up into his body, like the tremors of an acid-house party. Jonny shivers and turns it up. That way, the savage reality of conjugal life is spliced with the angst of the 80s indie slow build and the eventual thrashing could be either – two heavily-strung guitars on a wave of musical mutilation, or a wave of heavily-tattooed sidewinders directed straight at his Mum.

Pale Saints make Jonny think of Sean, make him feel like Sean, make him picture himself reading intellectualism, jamming and riffing Pixies covers and drinking with beautiful girls. They make him belong. On his own. In his bedroom. Ellie likes Pale Saints. Jonny knows because he purposely puts it on in the library and when she comes over to tell him to turn it down, she is instantly distracted by the discovery of a shared penchant. And they connect. Forever. Least, that's what Jonny tells Sean when he sees him in The Optic later that week. She has met the drummer. She says he is the drummer for Edsel Auctioneer as well and he lives down Cardigan Road somewhere. Jonny doesn't like the detail. She must fancy him and Jonny can't comprehend that. So he asks her about the words to *Language of Flowers*. She doesn't really know them. He can tell instantly when someone doesn't know what he knows. She is one of those annoying fans who hums and whistles over the intense clash of guitars, mumbling and blurting random words bearing no relation to the actual lyrics. Jonny knows them all. By heart. Just like he knows every sinew and freckle and blemish on Ellie's face. But he still doesn't get it – flowers cannot speak or write. They cannot use language. What a load of garbage. But he doesn't say that. He knows not to irritate Ellie. She has a temper. He's seen it in the library.

And so does Saffi. Saffi is Mum's boyfriend. Saffi is very kind to Jonny and he is very kind to Mum. And Jonny knows that Mum is happy because she is always very nice to Jonny when Saffi is there and she buys him things. She never used to buy him things. She buys him the earphones, for example. And she even lets him play his music loud on his stacking system. Sean's mates all laugh at Jonny's stacking system. Even the expression brings them out in hysterics. But Jonny loves it. It is walnut and the speaker wires are long, so he can have them all over his room and it even has a remote control so he can change the volume or whatever when he is lying on the bed. When Mum and Saffi come in giggling sometimes, late at night, Jonny tries to be quiet but Mum barges in and asks him to turn the music up and she sometimes dances ridiculously to his music with her eyes shut. And after slurring 'What is this rubbish? Yer can't dance to this', she bundles herself out the door and goes to find Saffi. And it's not very long before she is groaning on the other side of the wall, urging 'more, more, more' and then making noises she never makes in the daytime. But Jonny doesn't mind. He loves being bought presents and it's much nicer when he is not being shouted at. Mum shouts a lot when Saffi isn't there. So Jonny likes it when Saffi is there. Except that sometimes, like tonight, they row about Sean. Saffi thinks Sean is lazy and that these students are all sponging, whingeing layabouts wasting everybody's taxes and they don't work or do anything to help society and they just think someone owes them a living and they spend most of their time pissing other people's money up the wall and they swan around in the fancy car Daddy bought them, driving and texting on their fancy IPhones. They make him sick. Mum never picks a fight with Saffi. Never. Except about Sean. Sean looked after her when Dad left and if it hadn't been for him she would never have got through those years and he always had a smile on his face and he used to bring his little friends round and ask to go to the Dales and play in the river and it forced Mum to go out and enjoy herself and get some fresh air and it put a smile on her face and she just would not have survived without him. So when Saffi has another go, Mum gives as good as she gets. Until the sleeves get rolled up and the tattoos show. Then she knows it's gone too far. Then the other noise comes. Not the 'more, more' noise but the bones cracking and the chairs sliding and the thud thud of thuggery. And Jonny just hides away in his music, thinking that if only he could tell Sean, then it would all stop and he would not have to pretend at breakfast. He would not have to pretend not to notice the bruises and the cuts and the broken furniture and the satanic silence hanging over the Rice Krispies and he would not have to pretend he hadn't noticed that Mum hadn't tied her hair back. Mum always ties it back in the mornings. To do her eyeliner. Sean says that Rice Krispies are for babies. But Jonny likes them. But he doesn't like them if Mum pours the milk too soon because they go all soft and he hates them when they go soft.

It goes quiet. Jonny can feel the silence in the backdraft of *True Coming Dream*. *True Coming Dream* is barely two minutes of utter genius. It is a musical war with each instrument hell-bent on the destruction of the others. And somehow, a beautiful melody emerges and it truly warms the heart. It's like a shot of heroin in the midst of a mental maelstrom. That is, until the drummer finally conjures the Grim Reaper and shows the other instruments their fate. He hears Ellie telling someone all that and he remembers it, word for word, because he thinks it sounds clever and he is going to tell Sean or Dr Ramsbottom or even Grandad at the pub later.

'More, more… please… more.'

Jonny slips downstairs and out the front door with his music and goes to find Sean at The Optic. The line between pain and pleasure is blurred and Jonny is getting confused and irritable. He has to see his brother. He has to. Just for a few minutes. Just to calm him down. Or maybe Ellie will talk to him. Maybe she'll comfort him in his hour of need. And, after all, it is Thursday. And he knows exactly where to find her.

Chapter 13

Just 47 minutes til closing. The rain is battering the double-fronted doors of the Central Library. Ellie sits on the oak stool. Faffing. Trying to take her conscience somewhere else. Anywhere else. Trying to imagine a beach; a lover with soft, warm, long hands; a cool beer; an easy meander through narrow bazaars; tapas and the feel of silk on sun-kissed skin; an unspoken intimacy leaves her prone, deliciously deflated and ever so slightly beaded in his sweat; he slides from within her and finds a track she doesn't know he even knows, never mind loves; he melts the Afghan Black into the Rizla and roaches the joint expertly; the scent is sweet and saline and she is post-volcanic, molten lava running between her thighs; she is open, exposed, smoking; and into this sentient swirl seeps *Boring Machines Disturbs Sleep*, it is the fifth track on an album called *Happy Songs for Happy People* and Ellie has never met anyone who likes Mogwai quite like she does; a piercing, persistent, visceral, sonic stream of feedback deafens the ear, almost, to the layers of guitar creeping all over the track; and, rarely for a band which does not do voice, it is a gentle, soothing lullaby which unleashes a beautifully-plucked riff, only for the plodding percussion to wake you with a start, just as you think they are going to take you somewhere nice; it is intangible yet invasive; and it falls all over you like a flailing, emotionally-wrought drunk – I love you, I fuckin love you.

Maybe he'll come in. Pretend to be looking for a book. Casually leave his number on a library ticket and slink out, barely noticed. Maybe he'll ring the library to enquire about the availability of a very specific ISBN. Maybe he'll be waiting for her outside in his jalopy. Maybe he'll be at Pete's again.

Ellie is never introduced to Sean 'Beany' Hainsworth. He is just there one day, at Pete's, when she calls in, as she always does on a Thursday after the usual library shift, before going to meet the Doc. He is pretty. He is very pretty. He wears the drugs well and, unlike most of Pete's visitors, Beany is not wearing Fila and 8-Ball and Henry Lloyd. It's all Hugo Boss and his boyish, dark features and lucid blue eyes are not wizened or welling from the smoke and the powder. Ellie demurs, picks up her stuff and leaves, resisting, just, the urge to turn as she exits the kitchen down the stairs.

You don't go to Pete's for introductions. Pete's is not the place to acquaint, chat footie or chew the cud about the relative merits of Smith's economic legacy, Engels' blueprint for a fairer society or the flaws in Sartre's choice of setting for his existentialist piece *Huis Clos*. It is not the place for a social or a jamming session or an impromptu sleepover. People don't really hang around at Pete's. Pete doesn't hang around at Pete's. Keep movin, never stop never get stopped. That's just the kind of glib claptrap Pete would fire out as the door closes behind him. A conversation with Pete is like pitting a pre-Revolution Russian rifle against a latter-day sub-machine gun. Short-shrift, there's a definitive salvo and off he goes. And the replenished customer is left in a Sartrian vacuum, wondering where he is and what he is doing standing in someone else's kitchen with a bag of weed in one pocket and assorted pills in another, staring into a sink cluttered with a cupboard-full of dirty pots and a cooker whose spanking surface betrays a penchant for fast food.

And then one evening, Ellie calls in to find a gathering. And if she weren't so distracted and emotionally vexed, she would be shocked. Five students are standing looking over a snoring corpse on the lounge carpet. The only discernible sign of life, aside the gravelly rasp, is a twitching beard of amazonian foliage and a scratching right hand, frantically and persistently pawing the pocket on the ankle-length duffel coat. Pete says he left him there three days ago when he came for his usual. Pete has been away at a festival and has come back to find the guy still there. The bong is still warm, there are ashtrays full of splayed Silk Cut and roaches scattered over the sofa and there's a faint smell of piss.

'Fuckin tramp. Beardy's fuckin 'ad a bust-up with 'is missus again n eez lost the plot all over my fuckin gaff again. Ee does mi 'ed in, this geez. Shanty, Adolf, get 'old of 'is legs. We need to get 'im up the road sharpish, the pigs'll be all over this if they get wind. Fucksake.'

And the band of merry men brace and lift and poor old Beardy's on his way down the stairs, out the side door – to avoid passing Ali-Hamadi's shop front – and up the cobbled alley to his girlfriend's house.

Ellie is left in Pete's lounge with the gorgeous boy. And she makes a calculation: if Beany has been there a few minutes, he's had time to score his nine-bar. She knows it's a nine-bar because his skin-tight gilet hides very little and he was wearing it the first time she saw him.

'Should I wait for my stuff?'

'Pends how desperate you are. He still owes me the tabs and I gave him the readies so I'm gonna hang around a bit. Fancy a smoke? Pete's kitchen table is perfect for rollin a tight one.'

So Ellie meets Beany Hainsworth. Or thinks she does. And she's not rushing either. She should be at the bus stop by now but the Doc has wobbled on her again and she's sick of it and she's told him how she feels and she won't wait much longer for him and she'll soon be graduating and then she'll move away and it will all be over. And the Doc stops slurring obscenities and tells her he's sorry and that he's just found out the scale of the cheating at school and he's been with Mafe and he just hates his job and he feels trapped in a world of corruption from which he cannot extricate himself and on top of that he's had to put up with Jonny crying and asking them to stop shouting because his wife has overheard and berates him for being so bloody lazy and negative and miserable all the time

75

and then the Doc starts to cry too and he's pleading with her just to wait an extra 20 minutes while he changes the pumps and finds a reason to slip out...

Ellie and Beany smoke for ages. Sometimes chatting, exchanging rare tales of human and worldly eccentricity, wondering at the ridiculousness of situation and predicament. Sometimes silent, looking down, into themselves, out the window, at the sinkful of pots. Anywhere but at one another. And then at one another. They open the fridge looking for food or booze or both and laugh childishly at the paucity and the stench. They tell half-truths about relationships and family and A Levels and always being skint and what on earth they're going to do after graduation. It's all so easy.

And then Ellie just says it. Just like that. She has never chatted up a bloke before. She's never really fancied a bloke before. She's not really interested. All the blokes her age seem pathetic and immature and short-sighted and only after one thing. And the Doc had just fallen on her. Figuratively and literally. One minute he was reciting Hughes and Larkin and Owen, telling her that parents fuck you up, that poetry is as natural as leaves on a tree, rattling on about rifles and doom and deprivation and daffodils, telling her that he had no enemies but that his friends didn't like him, that the Gods had died of the plague, asking her to open him or readdress him like a parcel... and the next he was fumbling her bra over her head in the back of his car and, as Larkin himself might have put it, ramming it home in time to put the kettle on for tea.

But now it is she who is only after one thing. And out it comes.

'Will you fuck me? Will you fuck me on the table. Here. Now.'

And that is how she meets Beany Hainsworth. Or thinks she does. Ellie has just borne skin and bone to a half-truth, not realising that for every half-truth there is another half. And the other half may, or may not, be true.

'Excuse me. I said, do you have this in the second edition? My tutor tells me that the second edition is better.'

He is standing over her again. He does it a lot. And such is the insipidity of this sallow, pitiful stalker, Ellie feels like he has invaded her being, violated her in some way, even though there is a two-foot oak-panelled counter between them and a bric-a-brac of bookish bumph.

Ellie Barakowski has had this feeling before. The village in which she grew up used to house a satellite mental hospital from which residents were occasionally allowed out into the community. Over the years, parents and carers moved to the village to be near their loved ones, many barely capable of simple ablutions. And when Mrs Thatcher shut it and saved her precious share prices, an entire circus of psychiatric and neurotic misfits and malfunctioneers swarmed all over the few shops that had survived the economic cleansing of the 80s. And Ellie went into her butcher's one Tuesday morning to find a man in a sharp, skin-tight suit, Top Gun sunglasses and an attaché case handcuffed to his left wrist, ordering comfortably more than £200's worth of high-quality meat. Jim the butcher was affecting to gather the order but didn't seem to be packaging any of it. Ellie was perplexed, particularly when Jim turned his head to her and winked.

'Thanks, Mr Guillotine. That's great. I'll swing by and pick it up on Thursday. Capiche?'

'No worries, Mr Chelton. It'll be ready.'

And off went Mr Chelton, happy as a pig in shit. Ellie couldn't resist.

'Who's Mr Guillotine?'

'It's me, love. Gerrit? Butcher…choppin meat…. guillotine… he used be a French teacher, that geez. Went bonkers after a bad do wiya couple o sixth-formers int Dog n Duck apparently. Never got o'er it. Ee comes in 'ere every Tuesdi n orders shedloads. Never picks it up, like. So I never gerrit sorted… funny world innit?'

Ellie thinks maybe the library stalker is the one who got away. The one who escaped the village. Maybe he recognises her from all those years ago and maybe he's a lunatic and has wild dreams about kidnapping and running away with her.

Ellie is tired. She has just had an orgasmic holiday in the sun, met an 80s city slicker who orders a regal supply of meat from Mr Guillotine with no intention of picking it up and is now being bundled into the boot of a student car wrapped in bin bags and taken to a remote safe house in the back of beyond. And all the while she is rocking on an old school stool in the University library, ignoring a request for Lipsey's second edition in hardback.

'Thought you were studying Sciences?'

He stares back. Blank. He fumbles his papers. He mumbles something and nothing. She twists the knife.

'Lipsey is an Economics book.'

He goes back to his table. Bereft. Forlorn.

'We're closing in 15 minutes.'

The tannoy squeaks. Feedback. Mogwai. Marijuana. Manhood. He turns her over. Inside her. Warm. Slow. Slow. Cool breeze from the sash window. His exuberance drips onto the small of her back. And between her buttocks. He is over her. He is over. Done. Spent. She comes. Inaudibly. Imperceptibly. In the library. And the momentary lapse into sexuality seems to last several minutes. And all the while, Jonny is staring. Staring. Staring. And her contortions are like bludgeons to Jonny's head. What has he done wrong? Why is she angry? Has he offended her in some way? Will she not be his friend anymore? Did he break something? Did he use a big word and get it wrong, like he sometimes does in The Optic? And Grandad isn't there to take him to Curmudgeon Corner, to ask him to find a word, to calm his angst, to sooth his discomfort with a simple five-letter formula. He is alone. There are no words to save him. And then the doors open. And Jonny is asked to leave. And he looks for some sign of reconciliation in her face, in her words, in her motion. But she is stiff, expressionless, cold. Jonny feels like life is being drained from him. He sits under one of the great University pillars, as he always does. Still raining. But he is too frightened to follow her tonight. Too cowed to see her home safe. To see her into her dad's car at Highcliffe Corner. And he has to go and see Sean about Saffi and Mum. He has to.

When she comes out just a few moments later, Jonny watches her walk briskly into the distance. Ellie is exhausted. She can't see the Doc tonight. She just can't. He'll want dirty, perfunctory sex in the car. He always does on a Thursday because the missus shouts at him and he is angry. But she can't do it. Not tonight. It would take away the memory of that lovely orgasm she had earlier, on the stool, in the library. And as she turns into Park Road, she looks over her shoulder, ever so subtly. Strange. He isn't following her tonight. He always follows her. Always. But not tonight.

And a track comes to mind. Track 9 – the last track – on the Mogwai album. *Stop coming to my house*. And she smiles to herself. There's only one person she wants at her house tonight. And it isn't Jonny The Stalker. And it isn't the Doc either.

Chapter 14

'Gaz, what the fuck are you doin?'

'I'm in bed, for fucksake. What the fuck, it's only 'alf eight.'

'Aren't you s' posed to be at Shafty's?'

'Jesus. No, I texted 'er last night. I told 'er my eczema was bad n I couldn't wash the bloody glasses anymore.'

'Ha. You gonna claim sicky benefit after workin for three fuckin weeks? You fuckin flake.'

'Shut up, man. It's bad.'

'Dunt stop yer going out on the piss, though, does it?'

'Piss off. Got exams now an I can't be bothered with it all anyway. She'll call me later anyway, you know she will. She fancies the arse off me. She don't want me to leave.'

'As if.'

'Fuck you. Not my fault I'm gorgeous, you ugly twat.'

'Well you're no oil fuckin painting. I'd shave mi arse n walk backwards if I 'ad a face like that. You're just a bit of a slag.'

'Ah, get a barff. You're just jealous.'

'Like we all wanna be like you. You'll end up losin the power o speech, becomin a cripple n dyin of some hideous STD, like 'alf the French writers of the 19th century. N let me tell yer, I won't be there to push you round in your fuckin wheelie.'

'I'd still pull before you, even in a spazzy chair.'

'Huh... You want me to put some sausages on for yer? I'm a bit wasted n need a bit o fatty food shit.'

'Nah, thanks mate. Can't be eatin your Fulton's finest. Body's a temple. That's why they're flockin round man.'

'Jeez, you're ridiculous.'

'We got any bog-roll left by the way?'

'Dunno. But if you're goin for a clearout, write in the bloody book, will yer? You ain't written in if for fuckin ages n I need my memento when we're done. Finals are over soon enough n I might never see you again.'

'What so that's your memory of me, is it?'

'Well I don't wanna photo, do I? You're ugly mug on mi marble mantelpiece when all the glitterati are on their way round for a soirée. Don't think so.'

'Fuck you. Let's face it, they'll have to look at your moose-head anyway so it'll impress them that you know at least some of the Beautiful People.'

'Fucksake. Go fer yer shit. I'm on the Fulton's now.'

Pause. Silence. Padding feet.

'Oh and Beany?'

'What now?'

'Put me a couple on, will yer?'

'Aye. No worries.'

Beany pulls a bag of sausages from the freezer. The freezer compartment is so badly iced up that the bag has stuck to the sides and rips as he tugs, projecting most of the frozen sausages onto the floor.

'Fucksake. Do I need to get outta here fast.'

Beany stares at the floored sausages as though he's looking at the open grave of a close but only mildly-loved relative – sullen, pathetic. He sticks the ten remaining bangers onto a disgustingly greasy grill and lights a match under the gas. The blowback as the gas ignites almost sets his eyebrows on fire. And he steps back hastily, sliding further back as his Docs surf a couple of stray sausages. He flicks his Docs free of the spew and walks over to the Sony stacking system to peruse the CDs.

'Perfect.'

Galaxie 500. If Beany had to choose one band to kidnap to a desert island, instruments in tow, it would be a near-impossible heads or tails between The Cure and this late 80s three-piece. As if a guitar that taunts you with every emotion in its hazy meanderings, Jackson Pollock drums that desperately try to frame rhythm and melody, and a bass that soothes like a stoked, coal fire in the autumn chill were not enough, Dean Wareham had the audacity to cover Joy Division's *Ceremony* in the heart of Manchester, just as they were breaking through to a British audience tired of hearing of the latest 'New Smiths' and fearful of the all-conquering addiction of House Music. Beany had stood not a mile from Hac51 and witnessed this seminal gig. And from that moment, he would not be parted from the billowy breeze of Galaxie 500.

As Beany picks up every one of the 23 sausages from the scratty formica, Dean Wareham is telling us that he wrote a poem on a dogbiscuit but that the dog refused to look at it. And Beany smiles. He shouts up the stairs.

'You still in there, Spazman? Get on with it. Sausages are nearly done. N write in the bog book this time.'

'I'm just lookin now. Huh. Someone's written 'Chocolate, salty balls', signed Isaac Hayes, huh, that's not bad… huh 'Modest Clump', signed Tom Wanks… huh huh, oh fuckin 'ell listen to this one, 'I'll always be King Of Strain', signed Stinger in the Ringer… Fucksake, the last entry looks like that spaz Jonny's writing n he don't even live 'ere.'

'Fuck you, that's my brother you're talking about.'

'Yeah an he's special needs an he shouldn't be writin in the bog book.'

'He's autistic, you twat.'

'No, he's not, he's just a bit thick n he lives in a dream fuckin world. Your mum just wants some kinda special treatment for 'im cos she can't be bothered to look after 'im properly.'

'One o these days, Gaz, I'm gonna give you such a fuckin kickin. Not everyone 'as a mummy who'll pay for a posh school, only to find her precious boy gets 'is shitty little knickers in a twist about some pathetic shite an does a Reggie Perrin overnight. N then gets the mug of a woman to send 'im some money out to the Med so ee can fuck around in the sun for a while.'

'Bit harsh. Anyway, will you get a move on with those bangers. I'm out in twenty to meet a fine young lady for a peach schnapps.'

'Oh aye, what bird?'

'None of your beeswax. I'll tell yer later. Bit delicate at the mo…'

'You mean, she's wi someone else? Or married, knowin you…'

'Nah, some scouse nurse with great tits who's been tryin to dump her dentist boyfriend for ages. Like I say, mind yer own…'

Gareth tries to squeeze the spot in the mirror but he can't see his face. There's more toothpaste on the cracked glass than in the tube and Sean splintered the thing trying to swat a daddy longlegs with a nicked pint pot a few days back. There are still shards in the plughole and someone has shaved his eyebrows into the basin just for a laugh. Gareth just ends up nipping his eyelids with the tweezers and shouting f-words.

Chapter 15

Everything You Do Is A Balloon.

Jonny walks. The rain lashes him. The wind lashes him. The verbal violence lashes him. He walks. Lashes. Gran always said he had lovely lashes. They were wasted on a boy, she said. Gran is dead. Jonny misses Gran.

Sean will sort it. Sean will help Mum. Sean always does. When Sean isn't there, Mum only listens to Saffi. Mum does as she is told. Mum cleans when Saffi tells her to clean. Mum washes when Saffi tells her to wash. Mum irons when Saffi tells her to iron. Mum cooks and fucks when Saffi fuckin well tells her to cook and fuck. And that's that. And Jonny only listens to his music. And he gets through so much music that he has, over the last few years, acquired an acquired taste. He goes from *Message in a Bottle* to *Love Will Tear us Apart* to *Pornography* in a week. Mum has to go to the hospital by the time he's decided that *The Figurehead* is the best Cure track ever. He goes from *Disintegration* to *Come On, Die Young* to *And None Of Them Knew They Were Robots* soon after, when he overhears some drunken beardy in The Optic talking too loudly about Mogwai and then he reads something about German Metal in an interview on John Peel. From pop-punk to post-punk goth-porn to post-rock instrumental to death-metal in a month.

And for a couple of days it seems to have worked. Saffi isn't there and his toothbrush isn't in the bathroom and he doesn't hear Mum scream or groan at night and the tele is not on all the time and there isn't a smell of stale curry in the hallway all the time. But Mum is miserable and she cries all the time but she won't talk except to say 'mind your own fuckin business' and it's funny thinks Jonny cos why do people always take on their partner's verbal affectations when they split? Mum never swears but Saffi never stops swearing and now he's gone Mum is talking like him and when he tells Grandad Grandad tries to explain verbal affectations but Jonny doesn't really get it but he knows that Mum isn't happy when Saffi isn't there and she isn't happy when he is and he is lost and sad and so he goes back to his music.

And one day he goes downstairs because he hears a noise in the kitchen and he thinks Mum is home. But she isn't. It's him. He hasn't gone after all. So Jonny says nothing and goes back to his room and the YouTube track he put on has finished and it has done that thing where it just starts randomly playing a different band. And that is how he comes across Boards of Canada. They are a Scottish duo obsessed with Canadian TV or something and they play electronic music.

Jonny has a problem with electronic music – he is a puritan and he wants to know that the band can play their instruments properly and that they are not just sitting in their bedrooms with gizmos making up sounds and not really understanding music. If he were a muso, he'd ask all his guests if they could read music and if they couldn't he would refuse to play their music or interview them. But then he hears John Peel play Electronica and he can't square the circle so he asks Grandad what he thinks and Grandad says that music is intangible, ephemeral, quixotic and very personal and that one thing he does know is that the most beautiful art is inexplicable and that to explain it would remove its essence and sever its connection with the human soul and Jonny is lost again but this time he is not sad. He is not sad because he likes the music they play and he thinks it's ok to listen to it now. He isn't betraying music by listening to it. So he does.

Jonny walks. The rain batters him. The wind batters him. The fists batter her. Sean will sort it. Fish n chips. The batter has to be cooked in proper drippin n crispy. That's what Gran said. She would walk out of the restaurant if it was soggy, or if the bread was not buttered properly, or if the chips were anaemic, or if the tea was brought to the table too late, or too early, or if the mushies were put on the same plate and infected the fish. Gran called it The Fish Shop. Everyone else Jonny knew called it the Chippy. Jonny misses Gran. Grandad misses Gran too. Gran is dead. Grandad has his Sheppy, though. And his Scrabble board.

'Jonny lad, what you doin ere?'

'Is. Is. Is Ssssss. Is Sh Sh Sh Sean in?'

'Just gone to top up the Seabrook. We're out of prawn cocktail again. N this useless oaf does nowt. This place'd shut down inside a month if it were left to im.'

The Optic is funereal. Nails isn't happy. The Doc is reading behind the bar. Unshaven. Ruddy. Greying locks climbing all over his jowls. Bowed. Cowed. Nails can't even look at him when she's having a go. And the Doc, in turn, doesn't even flinch from his book.

'Yer know, we really have no idea about our own existence, do we? I'm readin this book at the moment about France in the 19th century and people would hibernate in troglodytic caves to suppress their appetite and save food. They'd wall up in late autumn and not come out til the spring. That's less than 150 bloody years ago. Unbelievable.'

Mafe is asleep. Nodding. Dribbling ever so slightly. The board is done. Near as. Jonny goes to sit with him. He sees words. Quiver. Triumvirate. Obsolescence. Joukery. Edentulous. Jonny smiles. Jonny loves his Grandad. Clever people always think they are cleverer than they are. They are cold and nasty and they use language to make Jonny feel small and stupid and pointless. Except Grandad. Grandad is kind and warm and he is not afraid of being found out. He is not afraid of being found out because there is nothing to find. He just likes words. If you cut Grandad open you'd find lots of very little people working busily and happily. Some would be stoking the hearth to keep the workers cosy at night. Some would be baking bread to keep the workers well-fed while they work. Some would be sewing up holes in clothes to keep the workers warm in winter and cool in the summer. And some would be growing vegetables and fruits to make pies and puddings to give the workers something to look forward to when they come home from work. And what would the workers be producing? The workers all work in The Word Factory. Grandad has talked to Jonny so very many times about The Word Factory. And that is how he knows that inside Grandad is just a good, lovely man. The Word Factory is the saviour of humankind. Without The Word Factory, the human race would have devoured itself long, long ago. Or that's what Grandad says, at any rate.

'You see, Jonny. As life has become more detached from nature and we have civilised, our instinctive, physical need to thrash out and hurt and maim and kill has seeped from our members and into our tongues and we just have this uncontrollable, inexorable need to find bad words, say bad things, denigrate and denounce. And the lovely men and women and children in The Word Factory have a very simple job – for every bad word brought to them, they have to find a good word, a word that will lift us, make us feel better, make us smile, laugh, feel good about ourselves, give us friendship, warmth, love. Because if we do not find the words to love one another, we will not be able to get close to one another and then there will be no more human beings and eventually, the old people will die and there will be no one left.'

Jonny knows that Grandad has read this in a book. The book is by a French writer called Erik Orsenna and Grandad loves Erik Orsenna. And Grandad is always telling Jonny to read it for himself. But Grandad forgets himself sometimes. Because the book is in French and Jonny cannot understand a word of French. Erik Orsenna wrote a book about water, too, and Grandad is always telling Jonny to be careful with it. It is precious, he says. And one day soon it may not come out of the taps anymore. In fact, in many parts of the world, it doesn't come out of the taps and the people are thirsty all the time and they die when they are young and they even have to wash in the same water that they drink. And there are places where there just is no water at all. And there are places where there is so much water that people can only live in their homes for nine months of the year because their homes are underwater for the other three and they live in boats some of the time. And Jonny always asks Grandad why the people with too much water can't just give the people with none some of their water. And Grandad sighs and harrumphs and asks Jonny to go and get him another pint of No3.

'Grandad, what does *Everything You Do Is A Balloon* mean?'

Mafe's metronomic snoring is disturbed and he draws his shoulders to his chin and gives a very deep, somnolent sigh. And then drifts back into slumber. Sean and the prawn cocktail appear from under the bar. Sean's complexion is the hue of the crisp packets – puffy and pink. It's either too much sun or too much booze and the sun hasn't been seen in these parts for a week or more so Jonny is not hopeful of a conversation.

'Jonny. Alreet, bud?'

Appearances can be deceptive, of course.

'Not really, Sean. He's come back again, Sean. Mum is making those noises again. And then she's hiding her face when I talk to her. I don't like it, Sean. He scares me but Mum won't talk to me.'

'Fucksake. As ee talked to you? Ee workin at the moment?'

'I don't really know. He disappeared for a few days n it's bin lovely but Mum has bin shoutin a lot n now eez back I may as well just go back to my music n all.'

'What you got on your wires at the mo, Jonny?'

'Oh, it's great, Sean. Pale Saints. They're a Leeds 4-piece an the drummer is drummer for Edsel Auctioneer n all. I bin listnin to this track called *True Coming Dream* n it's like a war between the instruments and then somehow a melody escapes from the chaos and it's just brilliant.'

Sean just stares. The moving mouth is Jonny's but the words coming out are most certainly not.

'You bin talkin to your little friend again?'

'Ellie, Sean. She's called Ellie. I told you. She's studying English n Philosophy at the Uni n I see her in the library all the time. She's lovely. She's taken my phone number n everythin.'

The Doc looks up. The rollercoaster has just dropped suddenly in his head and his senses are weightless. Bereft, he exhales uncontrollably.

'Ellie? How do you know Ellie, Jonny?'

Sean looks round at the Doc and overbalances, tipping the box of crisps onto the floor.

'Fucksake, Sean. They shoulda bin on the shelf ten minutes ago. Did you not get your Health n Safety Certificate, for Christ's sake?'

Nails isn't happy. And neither is the Doc. He thought she had gone out to the late cash n carry and his indignant response to Jonny's innocent optimism would have given him away. Would have. But Nails is oblivious at the best of times. The Doc could bring home a bedful of brothel-dwellers and she wouldn't bat an eyelid. She'll just hang fire til he retires and pays off the lease on The Optic and then take him for all he's worth. He so much as looks at another woman and she'll double her money.

The Doc's raised voice has woken Curmudgeon Corner.

'Hello, Jonny. What you doing in here this late? You should be tucked up and safe at this hour.'

'I just couldn't sleep, Grandad, and I just wanted to see Sean about something. It's alright. I'm alright.'

Mafe can see the whites of his eyes. Only, they are not white. They are a teary, bloodshot red. Mafe doesn't ask. He never does.

'Now that I've had my evening nap, shall we see if we can use up these last 6 letters, Jonny? Not easy because they are mostly consonants.'

Jonny desperately wants to tell the Doc all about Ellie. But Jonny desperately wants to help his grandad too. He looks at the Doc. He looks at the green baize bag. He starts to say something but it just comes out too softly and neither Mafe nor the Doc hear it at all. He sits down. He draws out the last two letters.

'A vowel, Grandad. That's good, isn't it?'

'It's very good, Jonny. Well done.'

Jonny looks over at the Doc again. He's gone to the other side of the bar, out of earshot. Jonny can't get up. That would mean being rude to Grandad and he couldn't do that. The Doc waits until his wife has left.

'Sean. How does Jonny know Ellie?'

Sean is confused. How does the Doc know Ellie?

'Err. She's some bird in the library. He goes there quite a bit to revise for his GCSEs cos he can't concentrate at home. He talks 'bout 'er quite a bit. Think he's got a little crush on her. It's all pretty harmless really.'

The Doc looks over at Jonny. Jonny is moving letters around for Mafe. Sean is pensive. He goes back to picking up the prawn cocktail. Derek won't leave The Optic tonight. It is Thursday. But his whole existence is flashing across Jonny's heavy, confused eyes.

'Grandad, what does *Everything You Do Is A Balloon* mean?'

'I am only surmising, young man, but I would suggest that it refers to the inconsequential nature of human existence. Everything you do just ends up floating away into oblivion. Nothing lasts forever, Jonny. Not even me.'

And Mafe smiles. And stares at the Doc as he puts an arm around Jonny's shoulder. The Doc goes back to his book.

Chapter 16

It's pissing down in the park. It's always bloody pissing down in the park. The light is fading behind the Falling field Building and Ellie's face is alabaster as the iconic old watchtower of the University.

Ellie often thinks it would make a great title for a northern version of T in the Park – Pissin Down Int Park, again. Ellie often thinks about the possible line-up and the food stalls and the fairground entertainment. There'd be The Buzzcocks and Morrissey, New Order and The Stone Roses, James and Elbow, Pale Saints and Edsel Auctioneer, Sisters of Mercy could support Pulp and Simon Armitage or – even better – Ian McMillan could read some proper northern poetry in the interludes. Frank Sidebottom would have to be shoe-horned in somewhere, possibly on the dodgems, and The Macc Lads could have a beer tent all to themselves. And in a lovely twist of revenge on those shysters Ellie cannot abide, Liam Gallagher would be on greasy spoon duty with Paul McCartney, serving up the culinary, regurgitated equivalent of their musical offerings over the years – namely, dog-burger with tasteless chips. The only people at their stall would be beer-bellied men so drunk they wouldn't recognise either of them or, better still, they'd be taking the piss out of them for being so pretentious as to look like them, without realising, of course, that they were, in fact, looking at the genuine article. Oh, and Noel would be sound-checking guitars for The Inspiral Carpets, like he did in the old days, before a few gerzillion people mistakenly decided that it was time to crown a modern three-chord successor to Status Quo. To maintain, you understand, well... the status quo. The stalls would sell Yorkshire Puddins n Lancashire Hotpot and the fish n chips would be fresh from Whitby and served up with curry sauce. There might even be a hologram George Formby headline using fancy technology. Although Ellie thinks that that may be incongruous with the lovely luddite image of God's Own County.

Ellie surprises herself sometimes. She carries these caricature images of The North around with her all the time and she finds an extraordinary humour in them. And she even meets people, almost every day, who look like the subject for Harry and Paul's next northern piss-take – flat caps, whippets, lamb chops, the lot. And yet, whenever she meets a fellow Northerner who exudes that completely fatuous pride, she abhors it, she runs a mile from it. She calls them 'professional Yorkshiremen' and they irritate the fuck out of her.

She draws her eyes away from the University buildings and starts – a fat, red-faced bus driver is staring right at her and wheezing something in her direction. His specs are so strong that Ellie supposes that, were she to put them on, she might be able to see the future, or even The South.

'Er you gettin on er what, love? If yer standin at a bus stop, people are gonna assume you're wantin a bus, know what a mean?'

'Errr, urgh, sorry, I'm terribly sorry. I was daydreaming. I'm waiting for my boyfriend to pick me up. Sorry.'

The driver mutters 'fer fucksake' under his breath and shouts 'What, yer boyfriend a bus driver is ee?', and he pulls out right in front of a banged-up old Micra and the even fatter lad driving that has to swerve into the outside lane and nearly crushes the pie he's eating on the rear-view mirror. 'Fucksake,' Ellie hears. The Micra has a sunroof. Yes, a sunroof. Presumably doubling its value. But Ellie doesn't really pay any attention to all this fucksaking. She's startled herself with the rather plum, educated tone in which she's delivered her apology to the driver. 'I'm terribly sorry' is straight from one of the many 19th century attempts at Bourgeois Realism she is reading at University; attempts which, all too often, are slow-drowned in waves of unrequited love and too many words ending needlessly in 'th', as though the biggest sociological problem of one of the most decadent eras in European history was, in fact, the lisp. All very ripe for mockery, particularly when the names Colin Firth or Hugh Grant or Edward Fox appear all over the credits. Suddenly, Ellie has become posh, aloof, haughty. And it humours her because it is quite incongruous with her parochial train of thought, which starts with Morrissey and Ian Brown having a gladioli fight over a Betty's Fat Rascal and ends when she realises that her grandmother, a born and bred mill girl from Shipley and a burler and mender in the mill all her working life, a woman who thought Bingley was in another country, would probably have hated every minute of 'Pissin Down int Park'. And her thoughts drift away.

Where the fuck is the Doc? He's always late but never this late. It's nearly half past. Fucksake. This has not happened very often. Derek only gets one evening off a week and he is usually desperate for a shag on Thursdays. Which is why it's always shit. He's finished almost the moment skin enters skin. He always says he likes to watch her pleasure herself afterwards but it's not the same and Ellie can't be bothered half the time. So she just sits there, damp, staring into the horizon, eyes fighting the swishing windscreen wipers and trying to make herself heard over the blowers. She should be relieved, really. Like she has said to him on so many occasions, the relationship is not going anywhere, he won't leave his wife, he won't want kids, she's got her own life to lead, she wants to travel and meet new people and be a student and do all the things students want to do and…

And yet, a bit like her yearning for quintessential northerness, whenever she has stared the reality of University life in the face – the grubby flats, the charity clothes, the monoxide fireplaces giving out next to no heat in the brass-cold depths of winter, the constant drunkenness, the juvenile coolness in pretending to do no work and yet get brilliant grades, the remorselessly upward momentum of the overdraft and the sporadic, split-second decisions (does he just want a quick fuck or does he actually fancy me?) – Ellie has demurred. She doesn't want it. She doesn't want to wake up with a banging hangover, a sore fanny, a fear of pregnancy and the dawning realisation that she has no idea who the bloke talking to himself in his sleep next to her is.

And the Doc has a maturity, an intellectual gravitas, a human warmth, a vulnerability that completely eludes the young bucks stamping and stomping their territory around her. He doesn't want her as part of some kind of rites of passage, a notch on the bedpost. His need is not egotism or chauvinism. It is desperation. She is the flicker of light in his dull, existential life. She is an escape from the drudgery of a career in which the most beautiful writers have been stripped naked and left like a rotting carcass for future generations to blindly revere, not realising, of course, that there is nothing left to say, that all meaning and interpretation have long ago been bled out of the corpse and spat out in classroom after classroom after classroom. Shakespeare is dead. Shakespeare is meaningless. His language doesn't speak to us anymore. Not because it's old. Not because it's too clever. But because the intellectual fascists have picked and unpicked it to smithereens and to read it is just to be used, to be shagged up the arse by a brooding 19 year old male from the Home Counties who can only think of going to the pub the next day and proclaiming his brown fuckin wings to the baying posse.

Where the fuck is the Doc? Ellie really needs a hug now. One of those long, goodbye hugs he gives her when he has to go away with his missus for a bit. Except he's not even turned up. Ellie turns to walk back towards the library, just as another bus slows and the driver gesticulates wildly at her, before veering back into the traffic to drop another load of boorish, whorish students outside the pub. The car behind beeps loud and long and then swerves into the lay-by.

'Ellie! Ellie! You need a lift? Hop in. On my way up to Pete's to score some weed. Where you headed?'

He's gorgeous. Fuck the Doc. She jumps in and turns to look at him. His thigh is prone on the clutch, he gently drops the gearstick into first with the tips of his elegant fingers and looks straight at her.

'That's weird. I was on my way up there too.'

'Well you were standin at the wrong fuckin bus stop then. It's back the other way, you dumb wench.'

'That's the worst attempt at a Northern accent I've heard in a long time, you posh twat.'

They laugh. Ellie needs a laugh. Fuckin 'ell Ellie needs a laugh.

'What you up to this evening, Ellie? It is Ellie, isn't it? I do remember right?'

Just the dull verb of the engine. Ellie is looking intently into the passenger side wing mirror. Gareth notes the unease but perseveres.

'Right?'

'What? Pardon? Sorry? Wh?'

'I do have your name right, don't I?'

'Err, yeah, sorry. It is Ellie. Nice to know I made an impression... yes, Ellie it is.'

'Sorry, I was a bit stoned by the time you left last time and I couldn't ask Pete cos I thought maybe you and he were having a bit of a thing, off n on, you know? Not sure I'd wanna get on the wrong side of Pete, if you understand me.'

'Me n Pete? What the fuck? What do you take me for? Why would I wanna get involved with that saddo? He might be a laugh but sooner or later you're gonna end up a prison widow with 'im. Besides, that wart on his face is bloody awful. It's got hairs growin out of it. He's grim.'

'What? Not even for a bit of free draw every now and then?'

'Bloody Nora. Wadda you take me for? Have you...'

'A bit of an 'ard-faced Northern bitch, now that yer askin.'

'Jeeesus. Here 'ee goes again. The posh twat from the Home Counties tellin us Northerners how it is… what a dick.'

'That's what the last young lady exclaimed when it got intimate.'

'Fucksake, what a pompous twat you are. You're Northern accent is bad as Dick Van Dyke's cockney in *Shitty, Shitty, Bang, Bang*. Have you conveniently forgotten what we did in Pete's flat, for fucksake?'

'Nice wordplay, lady. But it wasn't *Chitty, Chitty, Bang, Bang*, you twit, it was *Mary Poppins*.'

'Don't be ridiculous. It was that one with the bloke who wrote *The Railway Children* playing the mad uncle floating on the ceiling. That was *Chitty, Chitty, Bang, Bang*.'

'You're just wrong. It was *Poppins*. I used to sit and watch those films over and over on a Sunday when the rugger buggers were all out beasting each other or on the lash. I saw them all on an old portable black and white we'd smuggled into the dorm. It was great. It's one of my fondest memories of Chiviots – long, rainy Sundays watching awful acting, awful plots and cheesy screen kisses in black n white. Nearest we got to sex.'

'You go to public school?'

'Yeah.'

'What was that like, then?'

The lights change to red. His thigh draws down and back, the fingers ease the gearstick and he brings the car to an easy halt right on the white line. Ellie feels easy. Life seems to come easy to Beany. She has no evidence to back this sudden thought. It just drops into her head as he is pulling up at the lights. But Ellie trusts her instinct. She's not often wrong. The problem is that he is everything she said she didn't want in a man – young, arrogant, selfish, hedonistic, slightly misogynist. Intimidating, for want of a better word. Everything the Doc isn't, that's for sure. He makes her laugh.

'Tell you what. Shall we call in at The Pack Horse for a pint? You fancy a quick one?'

'That be lovely.'

'You in a hurry to get to Pete's?'

'No, not really.'

'You were never going there in the first place, were you, Ellie?'

The air hangs. Seconds are minutes. Lights go Green. Clutch, gas, distraction.

'Neither were you.'

'Touché.'

Ellie and Gareth drink a pint. They talk about everything and nothing. The conversation is punctuated with gratuitous expletives, flippant asides and industrial humour and the second pint goes down just as easily as the first.

Ellie tells him of her Polish grandparents, uttering inanities about the Second World War and persecution and emigration; and she tells him of the BJs at her school – Jewish lads who eschewed, to put it nicely, their religion, became very mercenary about their barmitzvah and called themselves 'Bad Jews' – BJs; they laugh caustically; she tells him of the village full of nutters where she grew up and her parents' divorce and her need to stay close to home because her mum is a bit of a basket case; they laugh about the butcher's customer and agree that the world of the spaz must be so much nicer than their existence; and Gareth mangles a George Orwell quotation from 1984 – something about Ignorance and Strength - only to find Ellie shouting the whole quotation over the top of him; they laugh at the communality and at Gareth's use of the word spaz and Gareth laughs at Ellie's description of Mum as a basket case; she tells him of her sense of isolation at school and the solace she sought in music and the English Language and her love of 19th century literature and her long, autumnal walks over Haworth Moor in search of the spirit of Emily Brontë; Gareth laughs at her pretentiousness and asks her if she met a ranger on the moor with a big dick called 'Mellors' and they both laugh whilst shouting hoarsely about coming off together, M'Lady; and she tells him of the numbskull called Jonny who stalks her in the library; and she laughs very loudly when he surmises that the idiot obviously escaped from her village to ensnare her with his lifetime supply of meat.

'That's just what I was bloody thinking.'

Gareth tells of being hit over the head with a concise Greek dictionary every time he contrived to score below half marks in his weekly Latin vocab test – which was every time; and they laugh about the camp-as-tits elderly Latin teacher and the pomposity of the mortar board and cape; he recalls hitting a master of French full in the face when he came to break up a fight in which Gareth was embroiled and Gareth assumed it was his counterpuncher's mate intervening; and they laugh at the thought that the Headmaster looked like Dick Dastardly off *The Wacky Races* and that the only time he was seen was when he route-marched Gareth from the building and suspended him for two weeks; he describes the sudden, long, final walk from grace and into the Auvergne to escape the public school chicanery and faggery and buggery; and they laugh at the comparison Ellie makes with Laurie Lee as she titles his autobiography *As I Fucked Off One Summer's Morning*.

But Ellie doesn't talk of her philandering father, with whom she has no relationship and hasn't had for eight years; she doesn't talk of her desperate search for a father-figure in her life and her utter submission to the English teacher, who would read passages from Jane Eyre to her after licking her fanny in a lay-by up at the Reservoir's edge; she doesn't talk of the dead-end relationship she is now in or the nervous nights she spends hoping that Jonny the Stalker will leave the library before she closes up; and she doesn't talk of the moonlighting she has been doing on the internet to fund her barely-controlled drug habit.

And Gareth tells her his name is Sean Hainsworth. That he is a Law student. That he is in his final year. That he is about to get a shitty job to fund Law school and that his grandad founded a Law firm for which he would eventually go and work under the present partners. He has to tell her all that. Because he has already sold that yarn to Pete to hide his identity and reassure him that he could pay back his drug debt – all in good time, dear boy. He'd heard bad things about Pete. Very bad things.

'You want another?'

'Thought you were drivin?'

'I can't drive now anyway – that's four we've put away already.'

'How are we getting home?'

'Where are you?'

'Park Rise, just be…'

'Yeah, I know it. Just off Highcliffe Corner?'

'Yeah.'

'I'll walk you on my way home. No worries.'

Since Ellie and Gareth arrived, groups of students have come and gone, many in fancy-dress and some in three-legged formation. Apart from the odd entwined couple, they mostly down one pint and move on. This is one of those pubs that never became a bar. It never pretended to go gastro, it never replaced its jukebox with a live-lounge and a DJ and it still serves hand-pulled hops into the small hours, rather than fizzy chemicals until the pump timer cuts out. You are more likely to hear Captain Beefheart or Kurt Cobain than Beyoncé or Taylor Swift in The Pack Horse and the bloke behind the bar is less poseur, more *Big Issue* seller.

'You into music, Ellie?'

'Now there's a tough question. I never like talking about music because I've come to the conclusion I just have weird taste and it just kills the conversation.'

The liquid has loosened the tongues by now and Ellie's attempt at self-effacement is quite disingenuous. She has no intention of keeping counsel on this, her most personal of passions.

'Ok. In that case, let's play a game. I list ten tracks and you tell me the artist and count how many you have either bought, played or desired. You do same for me. Keep a tally and loser buys the next round.'

Ellie smiles. 'You've got no chance.'

By the time the game finishes, Gareth is in love with Ellie Barakowski. But he is too pissed to sense that she wants him to invite himself in when he drops her home. And she is too pissed to realise that he has disappeared around the corner and not up the stairs as she shuts the door.

And the next morning he is too hung over to remember promising to take her to a Ghostpoet gig. And he can't even remember where she lives. He just remembers that she works at the library, that there's a bloke called Jonny who keeps an eye on her. And that he told her a pack of lies about his identity.

Part 3
Thursday Two Weeks Later

Chapter 17

Breakfast club. 7 a.m. Bright summer sunshine obscures the signing-in sheet. Jonny finds his name. Squiggle. He doesn't really have a signature.

An hour of nominators and denominators and numbers mixed with letters and improbable shapes looking like Edward Scissorhand's attempt at origami. Matrices but no Keanu Reeves. Not soup this time but gloop. The letters stick to the numbers like porridge to the ladle and Jonny chokes on his axes. Lucky that the paper arrived last night. And she'll be spooning out the logic before Jonny even sees it. Or the answers. Or both. Who cares? He just wants the treacle straight out the tin. Maybe swirl concentric circles onto the meniscus. Or penises.

Through the glass adjacent to the classroom door, Dr Ramsbottom can see Ms Wilhelm. And he can see Jonny Hainsworth. Ms Wilhelm is hunched, poised over the keys, straining every optical sinew as though primed to launch a missile so deadly and accurate that it would strike a minutely-traced target without the remotest collateral damage. She points, taps and clicks without once looking at her accomplice.

Jonny is mostly staring, nodding his head in acquiescence and ignorance. She moves his left hand along the keyboard with military precision and dexterity, like a piano teacher wristing the student through octave and scale. Jonny is limp, a puppet on a string, a flaccid, forlorn figure, utterly resigned and empty. Why say anything? She'll do as she does and he'll do as she says.

That is how it has been for six months.

Siobhan Wilhelm is taut, scrawny and ungainly. She is chinny and whiney, constantly rubbing her hands together like a Dickensian miser. She wears Viyella and it hangs off her like xxl on a clothes horse. The blonde highlights don't really hide the mouse-brown spaghetti, pale-blue eyeliner weighs heavy on the dead eyes and when her legs move, they shuffle, they drag like Grandma's slippers on a hospital ward. She's just fuckin ugly. There's no two-ways about it. And the Art teacher with the Enniskillen accent can't help himself, 'like shagging an iron board in a dishwasher'. Not that he would, of course.

Over the weeks, Jonny has learned to take himself away from there. He turns up, he sits down, he logs on, he waits for the wheel of doom to disappear on the screen and then he gives himself up. He surrenders his hand to she who must be obeyed. And then he goes travelling. Voyaging through his musical world. Sometimes it is Robert Smith screaming like a drowning man; sometimes it is Morrissey bemoaning the gratuitous and humiliating corporal punishment meted out by the 1960s bullying teacher; sometimes Mogwai take him somewhere nice with their effervescent feedback or Boards of Canada reach for the dead in electronic dystopia; sometimes C Duncan gently lullabies *I'll Be Gone By Winter* and, lately, Jonny has discovered a remix of Quantic's *Time Is The Enemy*, a beautifully melancholic chill-out tune hardened by D. Blaq's social commentary. It is all unremittingly cynical, self-pitying, faux-suicidal. But not to Jonny. To Jonny it is escapism, it is uplifting, it is essential. It is a relief from the mathematical muddle that is school and the emotional cryptic crossword that is family life.

But Jonny has to pass his Maths GCSE this time. He simply has to. And if he can pass a quick course in Statistics too, then Ms Wilhelm's bid for a deputy headship will surely be sealed and delivered. And, as a bonus, Jonny might get on a course somewhere, somehow. He may even stay at Highcliffe Academy. And the school will be able to add that to its overall figures for exam results and retention rates. And to its figures for students with Special Educational Needs.

So Jonny can take himself wherever he wants, listen to whatever he wants, interpret it in whichever way he wants. As long as he keep turning up to Intervention. As long as he keeps pressing the buttons. As long as he keeps accumulating marks. As long as he does exactly as Ms Wilhelm says. When she says it.

'Excuse me, Ms Wilhelm, sorry to disturb you, but I just need to get to my desk for a parent's phone number.'

Dr Ramsbottom has barely stepped into the room and Ms Wilhelm is up, out of her seat, hand arching over Derek's head and onto the door. She takes a firm grip. The door is ajar. But only just. And Derek is not getting through that gap. Or through Ms Wilhelm.

'This is an exam, Dr Ramsbottom. We are in an exam. If you'd take the time to look at the sign on the door, you'd have realised that you cannot come in for the next hour or so.'

The irritation in her voice borders on outright anger but, of course, Jonny mustn't see two teachers fall out. That would be unseemly. That would be unprofessional. That would be human. And it would be inappropriate. And in this school, being inappropriate is The Cardinal Sin. Because anything unacceptable to The Senior Leadership Team is deemed inappropriate. Disagreement is inappropriate. Debate is inappropriate. Unauthorised use of language is inappropriate. Emotional response is inappropriate. Unless, of course, you are a student at the school. Or, graver still, a parent of a student at the school. But Dr Ramsbottom is a teacher, a facilitator, a humble, pedagogical servant. So the door is closed in Dr Ramsbottom's face. The phone number will have to wait.

As will Jonny's musical escapade. Because the click of the door, the verbal battery and the palpable disharmony have drawn him back to the screen and the numbers and the discomfort of sitting so close to Ms Wilhelm. Or they would have. But Jonny is autistic. And Jonny cannot listen to two tunes at the same time.

'Do you like music, Mrs Wilhelm?'

'Yes of course, Jonny. Doesn't everyone… there we are… number 16, just have a look at the matrix, what do you see?'

But he can't detach.

'What does D. Blaq mean when he says that we live through our children, Mrs Wilhelm? What is he saying when he says that our souls multiply, Mrs Wilhelm?' '*Miss*, Jonny, how many times? *Miss* Wilhelm. I don't know what you are talking about. Who on earth is D. Blaq? We are onto number 16. We're doing quite well here.'

'At the moment, I'm listening to Pale Saints quite a lot, Ms Wilhelm. Have you heard them? They are from Leeds and their drummer is also drummer with Edsel Auctioneer. Their music takes quite a few listens but it is just fantastic. My girlfriend Ellie loves them. Do you know Ellie, Ms Wilhelm? She came to this school so maybe you taught her. I know Dr Ramsbottom knows her because he said he did the other night when I was in the pub talking to Sean and he seemed surprised that I knew her.'

'There are 9 numbers in this matrix, Jonny. They all have something in common, Jonny. Can you see what it is that links them all? Think of your times tables, Jonny.'

'We got talking in the library and I couldn't bear her walking to the bus stop alone so I sometimes walk with her and when her dad picks her up from the bus stop in his Citroën I know she is safe then. Well, I think she is safe. I have never really met Dad and I don't even know if it is Dad but he picks her up every Thursday night from the bus stop and it seems like a dad-type car to me. It's always the same one. A light-blue one, a Citroën. I have seen it so many times now, I remember the plate – YMO7 KTU – so if anything happened, the police would get him straight away.'

'Jonny, we were doing so well but I need you to concentrate now – we only have 17 minutes left and there are 4 questions to do. We can't afford to…'

And then Jonny's words catch up with her. Just in that moment. Just as she is about to launch another missile.

'Sorry, Jonny. I have just realised what you said.'

Pause while she clicks 'Save'.

'This Ellie girl? What is her surname, Jonny?'

'Barakowski. With a W. Did you teach her, Ms Wilhelm? I thought you might have.'

'Yes. Indeed I did.'

And just as Jonny thinks he has made a connection with this cold, calculating woman. Just as Jonny thinks he has reached out and connected with another human being in a very human way. Just as he thinks he might not have to carry on losing himself and all sense of self-worth in this mathematical maze. Just as a smile of shared experiences flickers on his face.

'Jonny. We are running out of time. There will not be any more chances here. We have to finish in the next 14 minutes. Otherwise you will leave this school with nothing and you'll end up sweeping streets and emptying bins for people who do know their nine times table. Now come on.'

And she grabs his wrist again. And the music lesson begins again. But not his music. Not the music of rhythm and melody and crescendo and harmony. The music of Ms Wilhelm. The music of a different keyboard. The music of deception and distortion and destruction and desperation. The music of the stealth bomber that is Wilhelm, hovering so viciously over her detonator. All day. Every day.

And in the end. In the end. Whatever beauty may be created by the great composer, it is all too easy for the manipulative conductor to twist it in his own image. Or, in this case, her image.

Chapter 18

Dr Ramsbottom is in the Head's office. Again.

There is a lot of glass. And veneer. And oh-I'm-so-busy post-its. And oh-I'm-so-popular flowers burgeoning out of oh-we-do-make-an-effort-with-our-calming-work-environment crystal vases.

An intercom radio crackles and squawks. Not so calming.

John Wayne is on the lunch queue. She isn't coping. John Wayne rides horses. Or shags all the time. Or both. And given that her prodigious thighs haven't met for best part of 20 years, her gait and stomp are pure cowboy. Or is that cowgirl? Mustn't offend Mrs Wayne, now must we.

The teachers don't realise just quite how much work she does behind the scenes. Oh how grateful they all are. Grateful that when a recidivist kicks and screams in indolent insolence again, she is there with her little room. Her little room, where crime and punishment are left outside and the cuddly toys and Connect 4 are there to make sure that little Karney doesn't bring his dad in to complain. Grateful that when one of them deigns to discipline, she has the presence of mind to remind them of their responsibilities, their professional integrity sacrificed at the altar of the great Church of Student Sensibilities.

And hence Dr Ramsbottom is in The Office. Again. Waiting for Her Ladyship.

Dr Ramsbottom reads the report. The lad is in detention next Thursday. Not that he'll be there. The lad, that is. He'll be in extra Maths classes with Wilhelm. Or at 'Collage', as he writes it in his school planner, 'faffin' wi' car engines n that'. It would be nice to imagine him stuck to a wall somewhere, covered in papier mâché.

He may have called Dr Ramsbottom a 'fuckin faggot'. He may have spat at him. But he's borderline pass at GCSE. And Wilhelm needs him. And anyway, he says he didn't spit AT Dr Ramsbottom. He just spat. Just to, well, spit. And why shouldn't he be believed? He's only a convicted felon with an ASBO. Dr Ramsbottom, au contraire, has never even had the audacity to so much as nick a smartie from his granddaughter's selection box. And he has given 27 years of unstinting service to his profession. But Wilhelm needs him. Karney, that is. Oh, she needs him more than he needs her. And she certainly needs him more than she needs Dr Ramsbottom. It's like a twisted marriage of Jane Austen and D. H. Lawrence. Unrequited pedagogy. With any luck they'll both come off together.

Oh no, good old Karney doesn't need Maths to go where he's going – some remand centre somewhere exotic, like Warrington. Nor does he need it on the off-chance that he makes it as far as Collage to do Motor Mechanics. But she does. Wilhelm, that is. And Dr Ramsbottom does. They all do. The staff. They all need Karney to get his C. They all need Wilhelm to stir that cauldron on their behalf. That way, Dr Ramsbottom may, or may not be, a fuckin faggot, but he'll be a fuckin faggot with a job.

Dr Ramsbottom turns back to his computer screen. It has just pinged at him. Detention duty in 20 minutes. Third one this year. Three more than Karney's done.

'Sorry, Derek, got waylaid, the lunch queue is chaos. Someone's let an exam group out early and they're giddy…'

'… Anyway, haven't got long… this trip… all very lovely and thanks for giving up your holiday to take them… how many are going?'

'87.'

'Ah, yes. Now then, Sheldon Metcalfe. Know he can be a pain…'

'He's been excluded, Mrs Berry. Twice. In under 12 months.'

'Yes, of course, I know. I excluded him. But it has to be said that the second exclusion was a marginal decision and only taken after Union intervention.'

'He assaulted a member of staff, Mrs Berry.'

'Yes, Derek. Sorry, can we calm down here, please? I sense an antagonistic tone and it is not helpful.'

'Mrs Berry. I am the trip leader. It is my neck on the line. Sheldon is a liability to the whole trip and his behaviour does not warrant a reward of this nature. I do not want him on the trip.'

'Derek. We need to establish one or two facts here. One, I am de facto leader of all trips and therefore it is my neck on the line. Two, Sheldon's deposit is paid and in accepting the money we tacitly agreed that he would go.'

'The reason he was able to pay the deposit is that your trip rules mean that any student may go to the finance office and pay without first coming to staff for permission to go on trips. I had no control over that.'

'Derek. He is Pupil Premium. Meaning that he does not have the social advantages of some of our more privileged students. If I refuse, the governors – and parents – are all over me on inequality and access.'

'But what about the rights of all the good kids who are going on this trip? He has no mates, Jenny, no one wants him to go.'

Pause. The bell goes. It's raining on the glass.

'Mrs Shaftsbury tells me he has been much better lately.'

Oh here we go… the long arm of John Wayne again…

'He was sent out of Maths only yesterday.'

'Yes but he turned up to detention.'

'Indeed. And you threw him out after only five minutes.'

The Berry stare. Dr Ramsbottom, yet again, is obviously to blame for the vicious circle that is Sheldon's behaviour. Come to think of it, Dr Ramsbottom is to blame for most things. For experience, read anachronism. For gravitas, read wanton abuse of privilege and power. Dr Ramsbottom's mind drifts. The rain is persistent, noisy. The genial slight on his profession that is The Smiths' *The Headmaster Ritual* comes to him. Perhaps Morrissey never realised that it is not only the pupils who are subjected to daily mockery and humiliation. He laughs to himself. This ritual he has indeed witnessed so very many times before.

Morrissey. Dr Ramsbottom loves him. But somehow, were he ever to meet him, the Doc thinks that he would probably change his mind very quickly.

'Derek, Mum has rung in today. Pupil Premium are covering the cost of the trip and he is going.'

'But he doesn't even have a passport and we go in 4 weeks.'

'I know. That's what Mum rang for. She is going up to Newcastle to collect it as soon as it is ready.'

'So she's ordered a passport on the accelerated service. That costs a fortune. Not to mention the rail-fare.'

Berry demurs. The penny drops.

'Oh, ok. Jesus. Bloody hell. And we're paying for both on top, are we? We are paying for the passport and we are paying for the emergency dash to Newcastle. Just so that a serial offender can come and ruin a lovely trip to Barcelona. And that's what I am giving up my holiday for, is it?'

'Derek. I am seeing the governors tonight. This meeting is over.'

'You know what, Jenny? My bloody family can't even afford a holiday this year. Know why? Because my wife is on compulsory bloody jury service and self-employed people get bugger-all compensation. So our holiday money is being withheld so that my wife can watch a powerless court release another common criminal back into the wild.'

'I didn't know you had re-married, Derek.'

Derek exhales audibly. He doesn't know what to say.

'Laughable. Bloody laughable.'

The radio squawks.

'Mrs B, are you there? Are you there? Shanice Wilson has locked herself in the toilets and won't come out. She's

screaming her head off about being put on second lunch…
she's just hungry, I think… are you there?'

Dr Ramsbottom idles out into the corridor. Two boys jostle
through him to get to the vending machine.

'Don't mind me.'

They don't.

Chapter 19

'Where were you last week?'

'Where were you the week before that?'

Ellie is already regretting not walking away from the bus stop as soon as she saw his car.

'Oh hello, Mr Barakowski. You don't know me. I'm Jonny Hainsworth and you don't know me. Just thought you'd like to know that your daughter is fucking her drug dealer every Thursday before she comes to meet you.'

'Shut the door, Ellie. Shut the fuckin door, fer fucksake. Shut the bastard door.'

Ellie shuts the door. He drives.

'That was clever.'

'Shut up Ellie. Just shut the fuck up.'

Last week, Ellie was in Manchester with Ghostpoet.

Well, not with Ghostpoet literally. Well actually, yes, literally in the same place as Ghostpoet, listening to him, watching him and, in fact, after the gig, talking to him directly. He jumped down from the stage at the end of the gig and embraced and talked to as many people as would dare to address this very warm, affable, unassuming poet of urban realism. Not that he would thank Ellie, or anyone else, probably, for labelling him in such a way.

Ghostpoet is not his real name. Obviously. But his expansive smile; his falcon-like wingspan; his languid, almost couldn't-give-a-shit delivery; his laconic poignancy in nailing the ambient menace of a simple bus journey, the physical awkwardness of bumping into an old flame, the desperation of serving fried chicken to the loitering yoot, it all seeps into you as you get swept along by the dub-goth, the hip-hop-rock, the eye-wateringly sharp quotidian observation, delivered as easily as a neighbourly chat over the garden fence. His unsentimental angst in the daily struggle is curiously moving, ephemeral yet haunting, cold yet rueful, contemporary yet nostalgic. And so to Ellie, his moniker is perfect – he expresses beautifully feelings that invade us unconsciously, that hover around us and in us from one minute to the next, day in, day out.

And Ellie feels like she has had a personal experience with this wonderful man, two of whose three albums have been Mercury-nominated – one of them twice.

Gareth surprised her.

He turned up at the library just before closing time. He ramped his decrepit rust-wagon up onto the double yellows and drove right into her evening, placing two tickets for Band On The Wall, very particularly, on the counter.

'Are you looking for anything in particular?'

'Why yes I am. I am looking for an evening in the delightful city of Manchester with a beautiful young lady. Do you know any?'

'Well as a matter of fact, yes I do. But she is working this evening.'

'Of that I am aware, dear lady. However, my information is that said lady is due to finish at nine and will be free thereafter.'

'Well, young gentleman, your information is somewhat awry as said lady is otherwise engaged until possibly one o'clock tomorrow morning.'

'Why, if that be indeed the case, I should have been more careful with my assimilation of the information and less presumptuous of your intentions, dear lady. For which I most humbly apologise.'

'Right, what the fuck do you want? You're a very sexy man but I'm workin an I got tings to do, know what a mean?'

'What's wid da black talk?'

'Ok. Jesus. Here it is. I'm closing up in ten an I got loads to do. That twat over there is stalkin me as usual an eez getting right on my tits. Meantime, I'm all outta weed an I got a date with a bloke I can barely look at later an eez gonna want to get naked an it's makin me feel sick. Does that cover it?'

'That seems pretty clear to me… Thing is, aside all the trials and tribulations of an entirely normal student life, you do read, do you? Ellie?'

'Fuck off.'

'No I shan't. Getting on ten minutes ago, I put these two tickets on the counter in front of you and you know exactly what they are, do you not?'

'It's not ten minutes. Nowhere near. But yes I do fuckin read. Band On The Wall. My favourite venue. And you know it is. But I'm tied up. I can't go. And that's that.'

'But you haven't read the gig, Ellie. Which is why I asked.'

'Oh Jesus. You won't let it lie, will you?'

'No I won't.'

'Sean. I can't go. I'm busy. Gerrit?'

Jonny looks up. That's not Sean. It's Gareth. He gets up from the Applied Physics book he is grazing without understanding a single word.

'Excuse me.'

'Closing up now. Please bring all books back to the counter and don't leave personal belongings in the library. Otherwise, they may be removed and destroyed.'

Jonny is approaching the desk. He is anxious. He needs Ellie to know the truth. He needs her to know who Sean – or Gareth – really is. He needs to let her know that she is in danger. That this person is telling her lies. And lies are bad. Grandad always said that lies were bad. They paint a false picture, he said. And the best art and the best culture is always honest, he said. A false picture can never be a true picture and therefore it will never reach below the skin-deep. He said.

But Ellie's stare frightens him. And he does not want to see her angry. Again. He has seen her angry once before. And that is once too often. He doesn't like it. Last time, he left the library with tears in his eyes and he couldn't see to follow her properly and he ended up bumping into a drunken student wandering home and getting a half-hearted punch in the face.

Gareth thrusts the ticket in her face.

'Look at the artist, you twit.'

And that's when the whole evening shifted. Shifted from a steady smoke, twenty minutes musing as Pete wanked all over her, a tired walk to Highcliffe Corner, a quiet, pensive drive to the far woods for a late walk and anal sex on the back seat of the Doc's car and a pseudo-intellectual conversation about the evening concert on Radio 3 or *The Last Word* on Radio 4 or Colm Tóibín's last recital at some nondescript church hall.

From corporal and cerebral prostitution to *Sloth Trot*, a hazy, reverberating meander through Ghostpoet's existential maze, vaguely looking for meaning, purpose, substance. From the screwed-up anxiety of everyday deceit and deception to the beautifully resigned sigh, the gallic shrug and the disarming disengagement of Obaro Ejimiwe, all washed down with a few lazy ales and a casual smoke in the dank Manchester sidestreets.

The drive over the M62 is cosy. Warm car on a cold night. Faintly-lit dashboard set against a tenebrous, moorland motorway where Mira Hindley buried her little boys and which seems to push the skyline endlessly away. Ambient dub mix on the player, irreverent conversation spliced with dark humour and cryptic communality and they're soon on the M60 and heading into the most vibrant, menacingly musical city in the North.

Band On The Wall is a bar and a dark room. And nothing more. It barely passes for a 'venue'. In fact, many pass by before realising they've missed it. The beer is cool and both reassuringly local and trendily foreign, the staff are dreaded and gothy and perfectly perfunctory, save the odd misfit student who is just so happy to be working in a safe and utterly non-sexist environment that she smiles permanently. The stage is dark and crushed up against the back wall of the adjacent room, and the bands Ellie has seen there are all wonderfully gifted at avoiding the charts and the limelight and the success-machine that is modern music. And they all seem so very pleased that someone has turned up to see them that they play their hearts out and come to drink with everyone in the bar afterwards. Ellie loves it. Ghostpoet's lead guitar is picked up by his mum and dad in the bar ten minutes after the gig finishes. He departs with a smile and two supermarket bags.

And Ghostpoet moves her, he makes her move. Ghostpoet makes her smile. He makes her laugh. And so does Gareth. And when they get back to Leeds, this time she opens the door to him before he can say no. And they drink whisky and talk about the student who got carried out of an exam last week, having climbed onto his desk, curled up in a ball and shouted repeatedly 'I am an orange, I am an orange, squeeze me dry, squeeze me dry'. They talk about the shitty world that awaits them after University, about the growing number of poncy, pretentious bars popping up all around student-ville and about *The Wacky Races*. Ellie always wanted the Anthill Mob to win and Gareth just wished Muttley would break from his shackles and run to the line to take an heroic, solo victory.

They laugh, he gives her oral sex on the sofa and they fall asleep in the lounge, entwined, slightly awkward when Ellie's anonymous flatmate walks in with her trainee management accountant swashbuckler. Neither Ellie nor Gareth has a stitch on.

Never mind. She fuckin hates her flatmate anyway and her twatty boyfriend made a pass at her in the toilet one morning when he stumbled in, so she put hair-straightening cream on his toothbrush and has not spoken to him since. She's just fuckin annoyed he might have seen one of her nipples before she covered up.

'Now what?'

'Well, you played a fine hand there, Mr Barakowski. God knows how that mental 'ed 'll react now.'

'Jesus, Ellie. You don't gerrit, do you? That mental 'ed is Jonny Hainsworth. Not only is he a student at the school in which I teach but his brother works with me and Jonny is always comin in The Optic to see his brother and his grandad, who drinks in there almost every fuckin day. I'm rumbled. Totally fuckin rumbled.'

'What the fuck is goin on with these Hainsworths? I keep hearin their fuckin names everywhere. Who the fuck are they?'

'The Hainsworths? How do you know 'em?'

'I know a guy called…'

'Oh, I gerrit. Now I fuckin gerrit. Sean is your fuckin dealer, is ee? An eez the one you bin shagging behind my fuckin back is ee? Makes sense now. A bit frosty lately, not too keen on sex, standin me up a couple o times 'ere n there. Makes absolute fuckin sense now.'

'Derek, for fucksake, let's just leave aside for one minute the fact that you are never gonna fuckin leave your trollop of a wife to be with me, that I want a future and a family and someone to share it with and you don't, and that you are shagging another woman every fuckin night and I am fully aware of that and have to deal with it. Let's just leave aside that I have to put up with your moods and your tirades and your miserableness and your constant bullshit promises. Meantime, I smoke a bit o weed, I have lots of acquaintances at University, given that I am a normal fuckin student. So fuckin what? And now I'm being stalked by a serial basket case whose existence is more Walter Mitty than Walter fuckin Mitty himself. An it turns out eez all over you like a rash n I was supposed to know that, was I?... Now tell me which bit o that can be interpreted as 'Ellie is a drug-addled whore who is about to drop you in it big time'? I'm fuckin sick o this shite, I really am.'

Silence. The Doc drives. Rubber on tarmac, distant sirens, backdraft of other cars, headlights sliding in and out of vision. The Doc brakes at the roundabout and engages third gear. As he releases, he moves his hand gently onto her knee. She flinches. Ever so slightly. Enough to make him feel a sharp rejection.

'D'yer think ee saw me properly? Ee didn't stoop low enough to see properly below the car roof and it is pretty dark at that bus stop.'

'Dunno, Doc. But I'm really confused because the bloke I know as Sean Hainsworth has not mentioned a brother or a job at The Optic. If he had, I'd have been very wary of talking to him.'

'How do you know him?'

'Oh.' Sharp intake of breath. 'When I finish library duty on a Thursday, I call by a bloke's house to get some weed – yer know, just enough for a couple o spliffs a night. The dealer's a nice enough fella and we smoke a bit while I'm killin time before I meet you. Nothing serious. Anyway, this Sean Hainsworth has been round a couple o times at the same time as me an' we got talkin one night cos the dealer 'ad a bone 'ed friend who needed takin back 'ome and we all 'elped lift 'im up the road. He's some kinda narcoleptic who keeps comin round an not goin home. Sean helped us do the liftin an ee seemed like a decent bloke. I liked 'im. That's all. But it spooks me cos if this stalker is called Hainsworth, it all just seems like a bit of a coincidence to me.'

The Doc pulls in at the edge of the woods. They sit in silence for quite a while.

'You know a singer called Ghostpoet?'

'No, would I? Does he do evening concerts on Radio 3?'

She laughs.

'Doubt it.'

Silence.

'And?'

'What?'

'Ghostpoet? What of him? Should I know him?'

'No. Not really. This whole thing just made me think of a track of his called *Us Against Whatever*. There's a line in it about how a couple share the same view on life and he talks about pork pies – as in the food and the hats, yer know the ones - n it just seemed to sum up how we are at the moment, yer know? Except that you're the old twat wearin the pork pie n I'm the young, unhealthy student eatin too many o the damn things. N who knows where the hat meets the pasty? Are we just not workin, Doc? Are we just a stupid play on words which means nothing n leads to nowhere?'

The Doc stares into the darkness. Why would he say anything here? Ellie sighs.

'Fuckin 'ell, I dunno.'

'Did ee write a tune with that title, n all?'

Ellie laughs. The Doc makes her laugh. N she loves him. She kisses him gently on the cheek.

'Will you take me home, Doc. Please. I'm tired.'

Chapter 20

'Bit 'eavy for you, is it, lad? Yer mate 'ere not 'elping much, I see. We'll leave him there int gutter. Don't want sick n bile int van, now do we? N' matter, our lads'll gi' yer an 'and wi that. Won't yer, lads? Come on, out 'at van, fellas, work time.'

'Not bloody students again, Jim? That sign is off The Pack Horse wall. That's theft, trespass, criminal damage n leaving a crime scene all at same time… that'll fill yer log book fer't neet, Jim.'

Cackling coppers, crackling radio. The eerie rattle of the back of the van. Nightfall. Waking hangover.

Police station. They take off Gareth's belt. He looks grim at times but you wouldn't have said suicidal. Procedure. He is wearing Beany's Ian Brown jeans – baggy, flared, white 501s. And they don't fit. So as Gareth reads out his full name, they slide nice and gently down to his ankles. He never flinches. Not one for undies, the lad. Attitude. Mr Stone Roses reeks of it and wreaks havoc with it. So they all do, these bloody students. They put him in a cell with a blanket. It's all concrete. Just like he's seen on the tele. Gareth lies on the narrow strip against the wall and falls quickly into a drunken stupor.

'What you studying, kid?'

Gareth has no idea how much time has passed. His head is banging and his mouth is furry. He feels vaguely nauseous but he could also murder a bacon n egg buttie.

'Law.'

Plod gives a disparaging cough as he cautions him for drunk n disorderly.

'Now best go scrape yer mate up off the road, n leave the bloody road furniture alone next time. The world doesn't belong to you bloody students, yer know.'

'Fancy orderin us a taxi, mate? It's a long walk back from 'ere.'

'On yer bike, yer cheeky get.'

'Worth a try. Don't have a bike anyhow.' He mutters the first bit but he only thinks the second.

Chapter 21

If someone were to ask Ellie how and why she came to have sex with Pete, she would not be able to tell that person, or anyone else. She would not be able to explain it to herself. But then, people do things all the time for which there is no explanation, rational or otherwise.

At least, that's how she rationalises it.

It is pretty simple. One night, she just smoked a few too many spliffs, got giggly with him, couldn't be arsed to go and meet the Doc and talk shiterature and console him in his umpteenth midlife crisis, and just ended up in his bed. She felt a bit rude and asked Pete what it was like to shag on an E. So Pete went to his drawer, swallowed a little white pill, gave her one, and that was that. It was as easy and as casual and as flagrant as that. And it was lovely. Consequence didn't even come into it.

Tonight, Ellie is not in the mood for sex. Not in the least. She has had a ticking off for handing in a lazy, ill-thought-out essay on existentialism by her tutor, a finger-wagging from a disgruntled borrower in the library and in between a bad phone call from her mum, who has been promised a visit for weeks now from her beloved daughter. Moreover, the Doc is being a pain in the arse, she wants to know what's going on with Sean Hainsworth and her period is late. Very. But Pete is in uncharacteristically relaxed mood. Presumably he's just offloaded another tasty consignment of gear and counted the thousands into his coffers. And it's awkward. Very. If she comes straight in firing questions about Sean, Pete's going to start asking questions. And he can be aggressive and confrontational and she doesn't really know where she stands with him – she assumes he has sex with other girls and she assumes he assumes she has sex with other blokes. But she doesn't really know what's in his head. In fact, she doesn't really know what's in hers. She just knows that she wants to find out if Sean has been lying to her about who he is.

They smoke. They smoke some more. And the conversation is so easy and flippant that Ellie knows that she is going to have to have sex with Pete if she is to get any sort of information out of him. A line of questioning now would be incongruous and suspicious. Pete is not stupid. And he strikes her as quite possessive. And he clearly wants to see her naked again. And in any case, she feels like it now.

They smoke just enough to start giggling at silly things. Like the big spider little spider hit squad prone in the top corners of the kitchen window, like the OCD cupboard of Pete's housemate, who in fact left some weeks ago and hasn't come back after confronting Pete about the coppers parked outside and getting an unequivocal, explicit instruction to mind his own business, and like the renaming of every Student Union in the country after a shifty South African called Mandela.

'Who the fuck is ee? Eez probably got ten wives n forty kids, the dirty bastard.'

Ellie nearly gags into her cleavage and tries not to look up too soon and force a response.

And then they hear the fucking. Old Narcolepsy in the room adjacent has managed to find himself a soul-mate and, according to Pete, has been shagging her senseless ever since. That is, in between long bouts of somnolence, of course. It is loud, it is explicit and they both seem to want to talk one another through every move, like they're recording an instruction video to be sold to bored, frustrated couples around the country. And she is apparently in some kind of surgical pain for which a good dose of Afghan Black would not go amiss, as Pete points out rather brazenly, with the intention that they hear his interjection. They don't.

So Ellie and Pete look at one another slightly nervously. And Pete rolls another joint and puts on the kettle. Ellie reaches up to get two mugs from the OCD cupboard. And Pete watches her bum as she does so. Her black skirt is a tad tight for her goodly thighs and, over-reaching slightly, it draws high enough for Pete to see the top-line of her fishnet tights. And that there is nothing covering her fanny.

'I can see your fanny.'

'Lovely. I can't reach these bloody mugs.'

'No, really. I can see your fanny.'

'Cheeky twat.'

'Just what I was thinking.'

They laugh.

'Thought your hair was dyed that black. Maybe not.'

'How do you know I don't dye my pubes?'

'Fair point. Well, do you?'

'No.'

And it just goes from there. Pete compliments her on her fanny. The smuttiness is juxtaposed with the sound of Mr and Mrs Narcolepsy reaching climax. And the flippancy quickly turns to arousal. Pete goes to the fridge to top up the milk in his tea and Ellie leans into him. They kiss violently. And then he suddenly relaxes in her mouth. He takes her into his room. He gently unpicks her clothes, running his hand across her thighs, her tits, her bum as he does so. And she lies spreadeagled like a whore on the bed and lets him probe and penetrate until he feels a rush of warmth. He slowly withdraws. Stands over her on the bed. And comes all over her. She watches his contortions. She feels his juices on her midriff, on her neck, in her hair. She smiles. He thanks her. And he steps over her, goes to the bedside drawer and licks a couple of Rizla.

There is a lovely, unfussy silence both inside and out. The odd car skims the tarmac outside and the sound of rustling cigarette papers and the smell of warm weed are like a lullaby in her head. Her eyelids are heavy and they close. She is not sure if she falls asleep or not but when she opens her eyes, he is over her with a cuppa in hand.

'You take sugar?'

'No, thanks.'

She sits up and sips. He draws on the spliff and hands it to her. She draws and blows from her nostrils in a single breath.

'Thanks. That's good.'

She stares at his bony arse. He stares out the window at a full reflection of the room sent back by the street light right outside the window.

'How d'you get to know Beany Hainsworth?'

'Beany Hainsworth? Who's he?'

'Yer know, Sean, the geez I met the other week when you had to carry your friend back to his girlfriend's house up the road?'

'What? When was that? Oh, yeah. What the fuck. That's the bloke you just heard shagging iz bird next door. Ee lives 'ere now – OCD moved out an ee was virtually livin 'ere anyway so I gave 'im that room for a bit while ee sorts imsen.'

'What, that's Beany Hainsworth?'

Pete is taken aback by Ellie's concern about Beany Hainsworth.

'No, not Beany you dick, Beardy. The narco who we carried back that night.'

'Oh, yeah. Sorry. Am a bit fucked tonight.'

They laugh, just.

'Why you so bothered anyway?'

'What d' yer mean?'

'You seem a bit concerned about this Sean geez.'

'No, no. I only met 'im a couple o times. Just seems like a nice guy.'

'You fancy 'im or somert?'

'Fuck off. Ee just seemed friendly that time, that's all.'

'So why ask about 'im?'

'I didn't. You started it. You mentioned 'im first.'

'Did I fuck. You did. You asked me how I know him.'

Ellie is trying to close the conversation down but she needs to know more.

'Oh yeah. But I didn't say I wanted to shag 'im. What d' yer think I am?'

'Well yer just shagged me, yer tart.'

They laugh.

'No, it's just that I'm not sure he is who he says he is, that's all.'

'Waddaya mean?'

'I don't know. It's just that I know a couple of people who seem to know a Sean Hainsworth and it ain't this guy. So unless there happen to be two of 'em livin round 'ere who are both students, someone is tell in porkies.'

'Mmm, that's interesting.'

'Really? Thought given your line of work you wouldn't care as long as they hand over the cash n keep schtum.'

'You'd think that. But if he's lyin about his ID, is ee lyin about somert else and puttin my little business in the firin line? N I am just 'avin a little think 'ere, an I were round Adolf's 'ouse lass week n some bloke I were 'avin a smoke wi said he wo doin French wi some geez called Beany 'ainsworth. N come to think about it, Beany told me ee wo studyin Law, cos ee ad a little bit o money owin to me n ee fobbed me off once tellin me eed get the money cos is family are lawyers n loaded. Think ee wo tryin to scare me wi the law fing.'

'Beany told me Law.'

'You know where ee lives?'

'No. D' you?'

'Think eez up the Tituses somewhere. I got a DJ mate up that way n eez on it so maybe ee'll know somert. I'll text 'im sharpish.'

Chapter 22

There's a track by Anglo-French collaboration The Crystal Method called *I Know It's You*. The video tells the story of a scarecrow who befriends a crow. He is tried for treasonable offences and imprisoned. The crow finds him in prison and, bit by bit, pecks away at his straw body and flies off to nest the straw on the outside, back in the fields. Eventually, he removes all the straw and resurrects the scarecrow in freedom. It is a fabulous, childlike tale of unlikely friendship. The power of it rests in its innocence, its naivety, its simplicity.

But the more the story is told, the more it becomes an allegory for something, a metaphor for something, a dramatic representation of something, a reflection of someone or something, a play on words, a semantic journey into pathos, bathos, romanticism. And The Dons talk of juxtaposition and symbolism and imagery and literary representation. And in trying to get to its essence, these do-gooders remove its very essence. They unpick it to the point of destruction, just as the crow does the scarecrow to get him out of prison. But, unlike the crow, these critical analysts have neither the wit nor the will to resurrect, re-create and therefore free the narrative. For that is not what they do. They trap it in an eternal prism of comprehension, they lay down THE definitive interpretation of it and will not be denied. They kill it.

Or they would do. But The Crystal Method do not walk the hallowed corridors of literary greatness, or even merit. Popular music is lowbrow and The Dons would not stoop. And so it is safe. Safe from the fate of Shakespeare and Molière and Cervantes and Dante and Brecht and and and.

But The Crystal Method do touch people's lives.

So when Jonny stumbles across them on YouTube after following a Joy Division link (from Joy Division to New Order to Peter Hook, bassist for both groups, to The Crystal Method, for which he guests on numerous tracks), he tells Sean of it in The Optic with such exuberance that the Doc overhears. At first, the Doc is startled at Jonny's lucidity – here is a boy who can barely string a sentence or a formula together in school, echoing his own enthusiasm for great art and, more poignant still, his views on its critics. He really does have to get out of the education system. And then it dawns on him. Jonny's words come straight from Ellie's mouth and the Doc sees not his daily bread sullied but a whole hidden pleasure exposed, laid bare among his only friends. He pulls another pint and goes out back for a fag. Beany just lets Jonny rattle on, as he does. And thinks nothing more of it.

But now Beany is sitting through a waking hangover, on a cold kitchen chair. He is hungry, it is late, he is sick of sausages and he doesn't really know what's happened to Gareth. He woke up on the cold, wet cobbles of St Christopher's Road, with a dribble of sicky, spitty stuff coming out the side of his mouth. He was freezing. And Gareth was nowhere to be seen. He has cuts on the palms of both hands and his knees are sore. He goes in the freezer. Bingo! Gareth must have been shopping. Fish fingers. Proper, BirdsEye fish fingers. A whole bag of em. He wacks six under the grill, puts on the kettle and grabs the computer on the side. And for some reason, the scarecrow comes to mind. And he types in 'Crystal Method' and finds the track Jonny was twatting on about. Tense, reverberating, instantly melodic electronica, sharp drum n bass interspersed with insistent, repetitive vocals and a techno siren seaming through the soundscape. And the video is brilliant. Shot in black and white. Close, angular, expressive and pathetic to the point of personification. Sean loves it. And just as he's about to turn the fish fingers, noise from upstairs.

Gareth?

He goes up to Gareth's room. It stinks of weed n stale sweat.

'Thought you were still ou…'

No one.

'What the fuck d'yer think you're doin'?

'Is Sean in?'

'Yes ee is. I'm Sean. Who the fuck are you?'

'Oh, fuck, you're not the Sean I need. 'As ee told me bullshit again?'

'Who? Who the fuck is this Sean and why are you on my windowsill two floors up, you dick?'

'I err, I err, I owe 'im twenty notes for some smokes.'

'Who?'

'Sean Hainsworth. I need to get in an leave 'im the dough.'

'What the fuck. I'm Sean Hainsworth. What the fuck is all this? An why would you break in to leave 'im money? Why not just knock?'

'Cos no one fuckin answered when I rang the bell. In any case, you're not Sean Hainsworth. Sean Hainsworth lives 'ere and ee buys a bit o stuff off me and you are not fuckin' 'im, my friend.'

'I'm not your friend… an I am Sean fuckin Hainsworth so why would you be standin on my bedroom windowsill two floors up?'

'Cos I owe Sean money.'

'But I'm Sean, you stupid twat.'

'No you're not. Sean lives 'ere cos ee told me ee does. Why would I lie when I owe 'im money, dick?'

'No ee didn't cos ee doesn't. And if you owe 'im money, why would ee send you to the wrong bloody 'ouse to collect a debt? N come to think of it, I'm 'avin' a conversation with someone standing on my sill two floors up tryin to break into my 'ouse… this is ridiculous… anyway, yer can explain all that shite to The Fuzz.'

Sean draws his mobile to his ear without taking his eyes off the window.

'Yeah. Hainsworth... 14, Titus Terrace... yeah... now... yeah right now... he's standing on my housemate's bedroom windowsill two floors up tryin' to get in the sash window... oh, hold on... he's just legged it down the scaffolding next door, God knows how he got round there...'

Beany ID's him quite well, he thinks.

'Fuck, the fingers!... errr... sorry, I'm burnin food 'ere... sorry... yeah... yeah... ok, thanks...'

The fish fingers are cremated, there's no bread and The Fuzz are on their way round now. Probably to show him a photo album full of black teenagers from the other side o' town. This guy was as pasty as a sickly Scandinavian. Waste of time. Nothing worth nickin anyway. Exams start soon and he'll be gone inside a month. Any case, if they do catch him, he'll probably be back outside the offy beggin for cigs n cider within two weeks. And if they don't, come to think... he'll be back outside the offy beggin for cigs n cider within two weeks...

Beany is thinking. He knows why he ID'd him so well... he recognises him from somewhere... but he can't pinpoint it. It's niggling at him. And he knows it's not the blond beggar outside the offy... And then it suddenly dawns that there's weeds n all sorts in the kitchen... and Gareth's room is full of pot n bongs n quite a few sealy bags... He legs it upstairs to sort the mess before The Pigs rock up.

The front door virtually bangs off its hinges.

'I'm com... oh, ello, what's wi you, Gaz? I wondered where you were.'

'Thanks for fuckin helping me out, mate. What a mate you are. Arrested, cautioned for DnD, humiliated in front of seven coppers, one of 'em female, n then I 'ad to bastard walk 'ome in the pissin rain.'

'The coppers are on their way round now so get your shit tidied up, man. I'll do the kitchen if you come up an do your room.'

'What? What the fuck? What they want now? They let me go without charge? What the f...?'

'Gaz, some twat just came round the house lookin for Sean Hainsworth. Ee was on your fuckin windowsill, man. Ee'd climbed up the scaffoldin next door. Ee was gonna come straight through your winda n ee didn't seem to gerrit that I'm Sean Hainsworth so fuck knows what ee was up to. Anyway, I called The Fuzz n they're on their way round so sort it n quick.'

'Sean Hainsworth? What? Well that's you, yer dick.'

'Yeah but ee 'ad no idea oo I was so eez obviously fucked up or there's another fuckin Sean H out there…'

'What di look like?'

'Tall. Skinny. Face like *The Scream*. Fairish hair. Ponytail. Nice clothes. Looked like a dealer to me.'

Gareth steps into the kitchen so Beany gets back to sorting Gareth's room.

'What you been burnin, you dick?'

'Fish fingers.' Beany is shouting from Gareth's bedroom.

'What, you mean my fish fingers?'

'Fucksake, man, will yer just get the weed n the Rizla n all that shit outta the kitchen. They'll be 'ere any time.'

'Nice tune, by the way. It's Crystal Method, innit? I think I've got this on an album. Think it's called *Legion of Boom* or something.'

'Gareth, for fucksake.'

'Sorry, sorry. I'm on it.'

'Will yer clean that bastard grill n all. Everythin I cook tastes of fuckin sausages.'

'That's you, yer dirty get.'

'Yeah but I cooked em for you the other day an you left a right fuckin mess when I went for that interview. Jesus.'

'Whatever. Where d'yer get this tune from anyway?'

'Old Spaz Jonny put me onto it. Apparently Peter Hook is involved with this lot. They're French n ee found it on a Joy Division link. Good, innit? Great vid.'

'Not bad for a spaz. He just listen to music all the time then, your lad?'

'Oh God yeah, not a lot else for 'im to occupy imsen is the? Cept Ellie.'

'What? Who the fuck is Ellie?'

'Oh eez in love wi some bird eez met at the Uni library. Obsessed ee is. N suddenly ee loves everythin she loves n ee won't stop talkin about 'er.'

'Uni library? How's ee get in there?'

'Jesus, you're as bad as the Doc.'

'What?'

'I give 'im my pass – it just gives 'im somewhere to go instead of sittin at 'ome n listnin to Mum shaggin or fightin wi Saffi.'

Gareth stops. He sits at the kitchen table. His palms are bleeding and his head hurts. A lot. Fuck. Fuck. Fuck. What were the fuckin chances of that? He licks a Rizla and rolls a joint. Beany hears the silence and smells the weed. He comes crashing down the stairs.

'Gazman, what the fuck are you doin? The Pigs are 'ere anytime. Fucksake.'

Part 4

The Following
Thursday/Friday

Chapter 23

'Need a word, Derek. When you've got a moment.'

Dr Ramsbottom has 60 reports to write in four days, a departmental plan to devise for the same deadline and he is teaching all day for the next two days and for an hour after school tonight to help 12 borderline students prepare for their upcoming GCSE assessment.

Borderline means that they could cost him his job if they fall the wrong side of the border in August. Three do not know or use English as their mother tongue, four have ADHD – or what Mafe would call congenital indolence, two are in care and used as babysitters by their foster parents, who are both seen daily in the Highcliffe Arms with assorted alcoholic waifs and strays, and the remaining three have barely a dozen brain cells to rub together.

But when Berry says 'a moment', well, she means now. And now is break. And break is 15 minutes. And Dr Ramsbottom has already lost five of them because he kept three lads back after lesson two when they started chucking water bombs at one another. And straight after break Dr Ramsbottom will be faced with 26 bottom-set Neanderthals who, two weeks from now, are going to be writing a critical essay on Shakespeare's use of language. Under exam conditions. Five of the borderliners are in there and the chances of them writing a C-grade essay are about the same as Dr Ramsbottom's chances of persuading the local council to allow a motley crew of locals to buy The Optic to save it from closure, or falling into the hands of one of the monstrous brewers of the world of alcohol. And Dr Ramsbottom hasn't really mustered anything for the hapless class because he got a bit pissed last night with Mafe, who was having one of those evenings of sorrow and nostalgia with which he is afflicted on a perennial basis. Meaning that he would talk increasingly pathetically and deliriously about how beautiful life was with his wheelchair-bound wife, before she died. And Dr Ramsbottom was up for a few because he'd had a shit day in the classroom, the wife had battered him for forgetting to order a new set of salt and pepper pots for the Sunday Roast Clientèle, Ellie had not fuckin turned up earlier and he was dying for a good fuck and, to cap it all, the Council had rejected his preliminary proposal to buy back the pub and the land around it, stating very clearly that the proposal did nothing to guarantee the imperative upgrade of the drainage system and that continual complaints from neighbours about lock-ins and noisy early-morning exits had not been addressed, quote, 'sufficiently robustly'.

'I've got Cara Shannon in Inclusion, Derek. She is absolutely furious that you took her planner from her bag last lesson yesterday.'

Inclusion is a room in the Behaviour department. It is where students whose misdemeanours would, in the good old days, have led to temporary or even permanent exclusion (or expulsion, as it was before the language fascists got a hold on our 'liberal' education system), are, well, excluded. Internally. So, not excluded then. Really. It allows teachers, theoretically, to get on with teaching, unshackled by the serious offenders and, much more importantly, it allows Mrs Berry to be seen to be addressing the issues raised without losing her impeccable 'Inclusion' record and without having to gather vacuous evidence and testimony to support an exclusion. In 'Inclusion', students sit and stare at a wall and pretend to do work-packs provided by teachers, teachers who invariably put any work produced straight in the bin and most certainly do not mark it.

Cara Shannon has made it her second home, to the extent that, as soon as a teacher deigns to request a modicum of work from her in lesson, she screws up her face in cerebral constipation and walks out shouting 'Am off t Be'aveya'.

There, she might cry crocodile tears, claim a range of unprofessional acts on behalf of the offending teacher with utter impunity and not a shred of substantive evidence, exhibit exactly the same behaviour to the Behaviour Team, again with utter impunity, tell tall (and believed) tales of academic and/or physical disadvantage, ask to be assessed for one or several of the myriad Educational Needs criteria (known in the staff room as The Litany of Excuses), or even persuade one of the Behaviour Team to play Connect 4, Draughts, Who Wants to be a Millionaire or Cluedo with her. The fact that the Cluedo game only has Colonel Mustard and Miss Scarlett left in the box would undoubtedly fail to dissuade her. In fact, the Colonel has had quite an appendage stuck onto his plastic torso using superglue (Jonny Debbin had to be taken to AnE after bringing it into school and sniffing it in a science lesson) and Miss Scarlett seems to have an unfeasibly large vagina and copious pubic hair felt-tipped onto the outside of her slightly risqué smock, making the game all the more hilarious for all who open the box.

'That would be because I did indeed take her planner from the top of her bag. She had been sent to my classroom to avoid disruption to another. She had verbally abused Mr Darshan and then she proceeded to call me, quote, 'a fuckin waste o space' and 'a bald-headed bastard'.

'Derek, you know that going into a student's bag without serious cause for concern is a professional no-no?'

'Of course.'

'Well, the problem I now have is that Cara is refusing to admit guilt, apologise or come back into lessons until she gets an apology from you.'

'What? Don't be ridiculous. She will be excluded for her verbal abuse of both me and our colleague, otherwise I shall seek professional advice. It is quite clear that a teacher does not have to tolerate verbal or physical abuse in the workplace.'

'Now hold on there, Derek. One, Cara Shannon IS excluded – she is out of lessons for the time being and at the very least for the rest of today. Two, how do we expect young people to accept responsibility for their behaviour if their teachers and other adults around them will not accept responsibility for their actions?'

'Jenny, I hereby apologise to you for going into Cara Shannon's bag without due cause. It was not the correct way to behave and my unprofessional actions have caused you work, for which I am sorry. There. I have apologised to the very person I have wronged. But I do not, under any circumstances, owe an apology to Cara. And further, I should not accept an apology from her even if it were given on bended knee and clutching a meadow of wild roses. It would be utterly disingenuous and I won't waste my time.'

'There we have it, Derek. Precisely the issue I always have with you. Any other member of staff would have happily held up their hands and apologised, thus allowing me to go for Cara for her utterly disgraceful conduct.'

'By 'go for', I presume you mean move her to another class and put her in a couple of detentions?'

'I don't have any more to say on the matter, Derek. This meeting is done.' Jenny Berry is on the point of combustion.

'It is indeed, Jenny. The bell has just gone and I am now heading to one of those classroom places, a place you have only visited in passing for going on twenty years.'

Dr Ramsbottom walks smartly into the staff room and takes his time brewing a cup of tea. The idle fuckers can wait. After all, a 53-minute lesson instead of a 60-minute one will have the same result come the exam – a total class word count for the imminent essay of under 100. Cumulatively. And that includes the names and essay title.

'Fuck 'em.' Dr Ramsbottom wanders back towards the classroom.

Chapter 24

'Fucksake, why's the door locked, man? It's not even lunchtime or are you fuckin Northerners on some kinda Mediterranean siesta or some fuckin thing?'

Gareth Simpson stares through the glass doors. She looks straight at him. He wasn't expecting to see Ellie behind the counter. She only does the Thursday evening shift. So he thought he'd come and settle his library debt before she got there. To avoid the identity explanation.

'Come on, for fucksake. The car's on double yellows and I've knocked off my shift early, you silly tart. I can see other people in there. Why are you ignoring me? What have I done to you, fucksake?'

She can't hear through the glass. But she knows exactly why he is angry. And desperate to get in. She had seen his clapped-out old Honda Civic ramp up outside and immediately drifted past the double-fronted doors and flicked the catch.

When Jonny sees her lock the doors, he panics. And he starts to shake when she circles the expansive oak tables and approaches him from behind. Ellie Barakowski has never once initiated a conversation with Jonny Hainsworth, except to ask him to put away the books, turn down the music on his earphones or leave the building at closing time. She leans right into his ear.

'That your brother at the door?'

Jonny fumbles his CD player, left to him by Sean when his brother got the grades to University and a celebratory IPhone Nano.

Thom Yorke is needling him, screeching at him, taunting him. Jonny is a creep, Jonny is a weirdo, what the hell is he doing here?

Shut up, Thom. Shut the fuck up.

'That your brother? Brayin the door down with the serial killer look on 'is face?'

'Nnnnn… no… no it's not. No it's not but…'

And before Jonny has chance to explain that the student gesticulating wildly at the door isn't Sean but that he knows Sean, in fact he lives with him and they are good friends but that he is called Gareth and that he sometimes tells lies but that he is a nice man and he was going to tell her about Gareth the other night but she seemed in a bad mood and she went off with Gareth anyway so how does she not know his real name; before he can engage Ellie in a conversation; before he can warn her that Pete is a nasty man and that she is in danger and that he would like to walk her home tonight to make sure she is safe and that she does not get Dr Ramsbottom into trouble with his wife, or the Police; before Jonny has time to straighten out his whole world and silence Thom Yorke, Ellie is at the doors, opening herself up to yet more lies.

'I'm not payin the extra quid ffs.' He actually says 'ffs'.

'I'm sorry, sir. I'm not clear on the state of your account. Could you give me your name?'

'I came the other night and you fuckin locked me out and you fuckin saw me at the door. It must have been 2 minutes after 9 and you fuckin knew what I'd come for. I pressed the fuckin books up against the glass and you just fuckin sauntered off in the other direction, wankin into the fuckin encyclopaedias, probably. I'm a fuckin student… you think I'm made of fuckin money… I'll pay the pissin fiver but the rest you can suck yer mum.'

'I'm sorry, sir. I don't recall you from last week – I only work on a Thursday.'

'I've been tryin to pay this debt for ages an you're gonna charge me for the extra days n I'm sick of these ridiculous library fines. It's almost as if you lot don't want people to read. I'll pay the fiver but not the extra quid.'

Ellie demurs. She simply cannot keep the façade but neither can she face a personal row in front of Jonny Hainsworth.

'You've obviously got more money than me.'

'What? What the fuck?'

'Well that car you just ramped onto the double yellas ain't runnin on sheep's piss, now is it? Yer know, my car's a funny version of your bean-tin – it's got handlebars, if you get me. So, like I say, more money than me and you are more than a month late. Someone with a brain might a wanted to read those. But they couldn't. Cos of you. Could they?'

Gareth looks at her, vexed, waiting for her to probe his identity. But she goes back to tidying and shelving books, as though he's not there. He throws his books onto the counter and tosses a fiver into the air as he turns for the exit.

'Fuckin ridiculous.'

The books on the counter are all over the floor and the fiver is still feathering the angry air, drifting towards Jonny.

'That date went well then?'

She laughs. 'Had worse.'

But the eyes don't engage. Like the doorstopper dossier he is leaning all over, this is all vaguely familiar but intangible. It is all unnecessarily complicated. Jonny is shaking. He cannot find the words to continue the conversation. He really needs his grandad now. So he leaves.

The book he leaves behind is the same one he always leaves behind. It is a book on Applied Physics and on page 46 is written his mobile phone number. Jonny Hainsworth has only ever read page 46. In fact, he has never even read that one.

Chapter 25

Siobhan Wilhelm is an obsequious bitch. Never to the needs of her teaching staff. Never to the needs of those who spend 23 hours a week entertaining, facilitating, cajoling, coercing and, heaven forfend, maybe even imparting knowledge. Oh no. But to the unconditional wishes of her fellow members of the Senior Leadership Team, to the indulgences of the ever more needy and excuse-laden students, to the wills and whims of a righteous and invasive parental interference, and to the potential for manipulation of examination criteria to better the school results, she is fastidious to the point of servility.

Siobhan Wilhelm is one of those teachers who came into the profession with the sole aim of getting out of the classroom as soon as possible. She did barely four years before she had her own office, a special title and a Personal Assistant. Much better, she surmised, to preach what others have to practise than practise what is preached. And when she is stooped over her screen, putting little figures into little boxes, formulating and formatting spreadsheets to prove improvement and the validity of her existence, Siobhan Wilhelm is like a pig in shit. And, undoubtedly, she is very good at it. To her, in her chiffon and scarf and softly-softly shoes, the names on these statistical plates of fool's gold, and the numbers that are forever rising and rising, propelling only Wilhelm herself to the kingdom of the Great and the Good, are precisely that – they are just names and numbers. And it is easy to forget. Easy to forget that those names and those numbers represent little people. Little people with doubts and deficiencies and devilries. So easy, in fact, that she has forgotten. And in her dealings with teachers, who might deign to suggest that certain students have, shall we say, certain intellectual limitations, it is equally easy to see how easily she has forgotten.

Siobhan Wilhelm is the very modern teacher – mercenary, workaholic and lacking any academic curiosity whatever. She has no intrinsic interest in her subject, anyone else's subject or, for that matter, the welfare of the students. In short, the intellectual and emotional arrogance know no bounds and no one knows who she really is. In any case, personality doesn't fit into boxes so it doesn't count for anything. But everyone knows what she is. And what she does.

'These end of year mock test results, Derek. A bit low, don't you think? You set the test, yes?'

'Yes. It was hard but quite a few did ok and, in any case, it needs to be – we have to find out who is going to cope next year. It's The Unseen that really does for them. But we'll get there. There was a 63/75 in Sally's set so we're doing something right.'

'Trouble is, Derek, the average was 38. And the History, Geography and Sociology grades were all As and Bs. And Notre Dame Sixth Form College up the road is consistently hitting As n Bs. If students decide to go there for one A Level, they'll take the whole lot with them and we'll lose numbers across the board. That's what happened at Highcliffe Manor and their Sixth Form died within three years, if you recall.'

'I appreciate that.'

'Bums on seats, Derek. If more and more choose English with other combinations, we are under pressure to turn grades to make sure we survive. You've been here long enough. You know the game. We lose our A Level, we lose at least ten staff, pretty much overnight.'

'I appreciate that.'

'You got a heavy A Level timetable, haven't you Derek?'

'Yes.'

'And I assume a return to teaching GCSE classes of 35 and the little darlings in year 7 wouldn't be getting you excited anymore?'

'Right.'

'So we are agreed that we need these students to stay on into the full A Level year, are we not?

'Of course. And I resent any suggestion that I am deliberately trying to lose students.'

'No one is suggesting that, Derek. Not at all. But no students equals no teachers equals heads on the block. And I know you understand that.'

'But we have 17 students in one A Level group and 12 in the other. Most schools would kill for numbers like that. If we lose a few now, we are not talking about Sixth Forms collapsing or teachers being made redundant. And you know we aren't. And frankly, if those students are going to go on and flunk the final exams, is that what you want on your precious record of results, Ms Wilhelm?

'But that's where you are not understanding me, Dr Ramsbottom. Like I said, they go from one subject, they go from at least three… and we know where that leads.'

'But that's nonsense and you know it. We all know that you'll just carry them for a year in the other two subjects, basically forcing teachers to keep them on when we know they are about to fail, just to satisfy some token tick-box, boosting our retention rate and keeping the income per student ticking along. Or you'll move them to another subject to secure university points and, again, protect your precious retention rates. And in any case, if I lose 5 or 6 students, that still leaves us with much higher numbers than most other schools.'

'Derek. Look. Maybe I'm not explaining myself very well.'

'Oh you are, Ms Wilhelm. As always, you are making yourself very clear. But just stop for a second, will you, and consider this – every time we set an essay question in English – Language or Literature – my colleagues have 29 essays to mark. They take at least 30 minutes each to mark, Ms Wilhelm.

That's 15 hours marking, by my primitive mathematics. And that's just one essay. The Mock is double the work.'

'Ok so you *are* advocating a deliberate reduction in student numbers then? You are actively looking to get rid of some students?'

'Ok. Enough. You're ridiculous. If you give me poor students to start with, if you force the numbers and inflate GCSE grades by doing coursework for weak students, we get dross, they fail their first year Sixth Form and we find ourselves in this situation. And there's nothing I can do unless we stop mollycoddling poor kids at GCSE.'

Ms Wilhelm looks straight at Derek. And sighs. A shroud of pointed sincerity comes over her face.

'Dr Ramsbottom, if we were to reduce the total available mark on the paper to, say, 65…and add 10 to each of the scores, to account for the severity of the unseen question, we would drift into A- and B-grade territory. Right?'

Derek just looks at her.

'That's just lovely, Ms Wihelm. So, let me get this right, the way to bridge the gap between GCSE and A Level and retain the world and his wife on every course…' he sighs deeply… 'is to maintain the same level of corruption and plagiarism at A Level as we do at GCSE. Right?'

'Dr Ramsbottom, please. We are simply not going to have this conversation because we are never going to agree.'

'So let's just, for a minute, sideline the immorality and disingenuousness of your proposal and look at the facts, shall we? Let's add ten marks to scores and reduce the total marks available. Three of my students, at least, would end up with 70+ out of 65. Now I'm no mathematician, Ms Wilhelm - and God knows how you doctor your figures in The Sixth Form to convince Her Ladyship that you are doing a good job -but that simply isn't going to work, now is it?'

'Who said anything about the top few students, Doctor?'

'Right. Enough. You people. You exasperate me. This is what you need to do. Go to Berry. Have a nice little chat. Play with your little Excel files. Massage the figures and the ego and your own senses of mutual worth. And write your nice little letter to parents. But don't expect me to sign it. Good day to you.'

Chapter 26

The upper branches of the oak are bowed by a heavy, early evening rainfall and they are obscuring Jonny's view of the sash window. Other than the occasional flitter and flicker of life, he sees little.

The soaked paving is drying in the summer humidity and the drip-drip of the trees shedding the shower punctuates the somnolent stillness of the post-exam student terraces. Many of the houses are now vacated and cheap, chipped boards are already stuck here and there advertising eight- and nine-bedroomed shared housing for rent. These streets were put up by Victorian mill owners to house working families of 10, 11, 12 mill-slaves. Now they house 10, 11, 12 indolent, pot-smoking students whose cerebral superiority will lead, in many cases, to call-centre slavery, domestic boredom, conjugal duplicity and a deepening sense of waste and wanton ridicule.

On a good night, he will see silhouette and contour from the knees up – the full cheeks, the small but perfectly-formed nipples, the full, homely thighs, her generous, attentive bum and even, once, the protrusion of her pubic bone. And he will see Pete's tall, lithe frame, almost shapeless from the side, his impeccably plastered ponytail, his slightly oversized nose and even the hollow of his drug-drawn jawline. Jonny thinks of those awful Biology lessons in which he was made to stand at the front and point to skeletal bones and joints as they were shouted out by classmates, one or two of whom would inevitably shout 'twat', 'cunt', 'shithole' or some other inanity and be sent out to have a good giggle about it with John Wayne in Behaviour. And his large, erect penis leaves Jonny in no doubt as it merges with Ellie's facial form, or her pelvic thrust, or even her draped torso, prone over what Jonny imagines to be a beautiful silk sheet.

But tonight he sees little. As usual, there is a strong smell of weed hanging over the tiny front garden and Pete opens the door almost the second she knocks, drawing her immediately to him for a mealy-mouthed snog. They appear in the kitchen for a short while and Jonny can feel the deep bass-line of an anthemic mix. He thinks he recognises a *Ministry of Sound* CD – Chicane's Saltwater is too subliminal to be picked out at that distance but Jonny seems to remember it having an unmistakeable Enya sample running through it and he keeps getting wafts of that plaintive Celtic lushness. The bedroom light goes on after about 20 minutes. But it is a very brief illumination before Ellie re-appears at the front door, faffing in her fashionably big bag to find yet another drug – her mobile. She texts as she negotiates the rotten wooden gate, hanging it back on its rusty hinges before turning up the hill towards the park road.

Jonny has stepped back into the shadows to maintain the charade. She knows he's there. He knows that she knows he's there. And she knows that he knows that she knows he's there. And the text to the Doc allows her to pretend that she doesn't notice him and make her way up Carsley Crescent and left onto the park road. As always, she glances to the side as she turns left to make sure he is there but at a safe distance. He will be. He always is.

Except that, this time, he is not. Ellie stops dead. Her jaw is dropped and she scours the street for a view of him. Nothing. Nobody. And then she shifts her sightline left and over the street, back to Pete's. Jonny is struggling with the garden gate. He is going to Pete's door. He is going to see Pete.

What the fuck is ee doing now?

Ellie is furious. What the fuckin 'ell does ee think eez doin? Is ee intent on invadin every aspect of 'er fuckin life now? She's gonna have to go to the police about this shit. It's gettin bloody unnervin n she can't go anywhere or do anythin without that weirdo houndin 'er like a fuckin scented fuckin fox. It's just. It's just. Well, it's just what if they start askin awkward fuckin questions like about the Doc n Pete n the drug-takin n the sordid sex life she leads n. N well, n now she comes to think about it, they won't aff to scratch far below the fuckin surface to expose 'er deviance n decadence. N she'll end up lookin more ridiculous than 'im, not to mention the fact that the Doc 'll get put on some register n Pete 'll go down for a least a couple o years. Fucksake, there's 'alf o the Colombian drug plantation in Pete's breadbin alone. Any case, she needs to get to the Doc tonight. She needs to sort it once n for all. It ain't goin anywhere, she's sick of iz moods n iz mannerisms n iz mumblin, mollycoddlin mitherins n she juss wants peace, 'er books, 'er music, good drugs n proper sex n no complications. She doesn't wanna skulk around, duck n dive, deny 'erself a student life just for a shit shag in the back of a dusty old Picasso n some regurgitated old literary insight she could get from any old net-page. Fuck it. She deserves better. Much fuckin better.

Ellie is furious. But Ellie is alone. And helpless. Disoriented. And she's got the faintest taste of marijuana n semen in 'er mouth n a damp fanny. She certainly doesn't wanna see the Doc's miserable face but she can't go back to Pete's n expose a whole loada shit. Thinkin about it, she can always dismiss Jonny's ramblins later as those of an isolated freak. But if she goes back down there now, she pretty much admits to everythin. She's dead in the water. So Ellie walks on. No goin back now. What's done is done. Fair is foul n foul is fuckin fair. If t'were done when tis bloody done, then t'were well t'were bloody done quickly.

And that sudden invasion of Shakespeare irritates her even more. It's like a slow, drip-fed indoctrination, almost as soon as we are old enough to read. William fuckin Shakespeare. The man with a pithy quote to cover every bloody situation, every fuckin emotion, every twist of friggin sobriety. Yer just can't get away from the twit. And as she walks purposefully towards Highcliffe Corner, Ellie ponders the irony of Lady Macbeth and her damned spots and her guilt-driven paranoia. She cannot escape her own mind, just like we cannot escape his bloody writings. Shakespeare is great just as surely as Duncan is dead. And denial will only lead to isolation and self-destruction. He's inescapable. For fucksake, Shakespeare wrote about our fuckin lives before we even led them. He taught us lessons 400 bloody years before we were alive to learn them. What a presumptuous, pompous, polymorphic pervert. Yes, he perverted the course of human existence even before its path was chosen. If ever there was a case for Nietzsche, William Shakespeare is most definitely it.

She walks. She walks. It's spittin again. Fucksake.

Jonny knocks at the door. A calculating coldness has just driven straight through his head. This man is horrible. This man is illegal. This man is destructive. This man will take Ellie down with him. This man is sullying the purity of his beautiful woman. This man cannot be allowed to get away with it. Any of it. But before the police get to him, Jonny wants to right the wrongs, read the riot act, settle the score.

'Who the fuck are you?'

'Wou... wou... would you mind if I come in. Please?'

Pete smirks. He has no idea who this guy is. Or what he might want. He's never clapped eyes on him in his life. And, frankly, he doesn't look like the sort who'd be knocking at his door for the kind of services he offers. But Pete is a bit doped. And he's met all sorts. And at the very least, he figures, he can have some fun with this fella. He's not doing a right lot else.

Jonny stands in the kitchen doorway. He has to be asked to sit down. He has to be asked if he wants a drink. He has to be asked how much milk he wants in his tea, whether or not he wants milk at all, in fact. He has to be asked to sit down. Again. He has to be asked what he wants. He has to be asked why he has come. And he has to be asked to sit down. Again. Jonny says please and thank you and just a drop and then he tries to explain to Pete why the common expression 'a bit of milk' is grammatically incorrect. And when Pete says 'less cups', Jonny corrects him – 'fewer'. 'What?' And Jonny repeats the word fewer and explains why the word fewer is more appropriate here. And very quickly Pete realises that there is little fun to be had with this urchin.

'What the fuck do you want? I'm kinda pushed for time, yer know?'

And Jonny can't think of anything. He is trapped. He has come to a flat which is wholly unfamiliar to see a person whose personality is more a mystery to him than his penis. He has no real motive for being there and he feels verbally and physically threatened by the constant sardonic look on Pete's face. But Jonny cannot sit in silence indefinitely. And now he needs to get out.

'Look, mate. I'm really not sure why you knocked on my door. Yer know what, I'm all for socialisin n mekkin new friends n that. I'm even up for the odd surreal experience, if yer get mi drift. But a silent vigil wi a complete fuckin stranger in mi own kitchin. Not sure what I'd be getting out of it. D' yer get mi?'

Jonny is shaking. Jonny is shaking a lot. Jonny looks cold. But Jonny is hot. Very hot. And his palms are slippery on the mug. It drops, almost in slow motion, onto the wooden floor. His hands flail to arrest the fall. No chance. Tea flies out in all directions and splatters the fridge, the microwave, the table, Pete's face. Pete stays completely still, unable to rationalise the experience he is having. How much dope has he smoked? Maybe it's getting outta hand... huh... outta hand... gerrit? When he comes out of his own head, Pete is aggravated.

'Look mate. If you need your methadone fix, you need get down the chemist sharpish. The one on Park Road is open this time on a night, I think.'

'I need 3 Es n 3 wraps o whizz. Please.'

Pete stares. Those words did not come out of Jonny's mouth. This joker does not know what he has just asked for.

'What's yer name, son?'

'Jonny. N I'm not your son.'

Pete smiles. Pause. Jonny looks down.

'Jonny what?'

'Hainsworth, what's it to you? Can you supply me or not? If not, I'll go somewhere else. Or maybe I'll go have a word with that policeman who's parked at the top of the road.'

Pete stops. He rocks back in his chair. He's nearly violent with anger but something checks his fist as it braces.

'Hainsworth? Hainsworth? Don't I know a Hainsworth?'

'Possibly. My brother.'

'Hainsworth. Hainsworth. Fuckin 'ell, aye. Ee comes 'ere for a score every Thursday. Nice geez. Dunt look fuckall like you, man. Fuckin ell, maybe you can tell mi this then, is ee shagging someone at the mo? Someone called Ellie?'

'No. He doesn't have a girlfriend and he doesn't get 'is drugs from you either. He gets 'em from Gareth Simpson. N by the way, Gareth Simpson is fuckin your Ellie. Ee took 'er to see Ghostpoet last week n they went back to 'er place for the whole night. N while we're on it, she's bin seein a teacher from my school in secret for months. She meets 'im at Highcliffe Corner after she comes 'ere every Thursday night. She thinks I think it's 'er dad pickin 'er up in 'is Picasso but it isn't. He's an English teacher at my school n he runs The Optic.'

Pete's face doesn't flicker. Pokerface Pete. Has to be, in his line of work.

'Ghostpoet. Nice choice. Shit for business, though. Eez a bit God-squaddy an loads of 'is people are too fuckin middle-class twee to buy from me. Still, can't knock the music.'

Jonny didn't mean to say all that. He really did not mean to say all that. Not the bit about the E's n the whizz. He meant that. He's heard Sean ask for that n he can just give the drugs to him. The bit about Ellie. He has always known, really, that she was meeting an older man at the park. He has always known that Ellie had a secret life. And he has always known about Dr Ramsbottom's secret life too. And, until now, he has had no reason to reveal the secret. He loves Ellie too much and would much rather she were in the hands of an older man known to him because, one, he knows she will be looked after and two, he knows that one day it will end and that he, Jonny, will be there to pick up the pieces. And he loves Dr

154

Ramsbottom. Because he looks after him at school and sometimes in The Optic and he is like a father to Jonny and he looks after Jonny's grandad, Mafe, in the pub and generally. It was all very neat. All very nice. All very controlled. Until now. Until he realised that Ellie had more than one secret life. And now he cannot stop shaking. He shakes all the time. His world is collapsing all around him and he can't even go home to calm down and get a sense of perspective cos all he gets is Mum either riding roughshod over him or riding her fuckin hideous boyfriend. Jonny's face tells pretty much this whole story. Pete needs rid. Quickly.

'Here, fella. That'll be 150 notes to you.'

Jonny goes into his pocket and takes out the £200 Grandad gave him to give to Sean for his debts.

'I'd tek one o those now if I were you, fella. Yer look as though yer need it.'

And by the time Jonny comes to terms with his own stupidity. By the time he realises that he has just breached the trust that Ellie never put in him. By the time he realises that he has compromised his favourite teacher. And by the time he realises that he has just put one of the white tablets in his mouth and swilled it down with a mouthful of tea, just like Mum does with the Nurofen, Pete is gone. Out the door, up the road. Running straight past the police car and left onto the park road.

Jonny hesitates. He sits a minute. Waiting for the drug to take effect. Expecting an immediate out-of-body experience. Nothing. Nothing at all. So he gets up and goes after Pete.

What's Pete gonna do? Shit, has he gone after Ellie?

Chapter 27

'Marxize ain't a word, you silly old git.'

'Yes it bloody well is. Thought you were an English teacher.'

'Precisely. Economics and History and Political Theory are distant memories but I'm pretty sure that marxize is not in the OED.'

'Well if you would care to go and fetch it, young whipper, I think you'll find that it has two meanings – to adapt in accordance with Marxist doctrine or to advocate Marxism. But before you do, put another in there, will yer?'

'Aye.'

The Doc takes the pint pot and goes back behind the long, oak bar. The solid-soled shoes echo on the polished wooden floor. He pulls on the pump and watches Mafe scour the board and the remaining letters. A man at peace. And it is peaceful. There's only Mafe in and the tick tock of the grandfather clock – which had indeed belonged to the Doc's grandfather, the rhythmic clunk of the hand-pull and the tap tap tap of the old wooden letters on the board are the only sounds to be heard. Beany is pottering: clearing the back room for a rare gig the following night; cleaning pumps and pipes; filling crisp boxes and condiment pots; updating the community information board. Just doing stuff, really.

The Doc is contented. Schools and pubs are such noisy places and tranquillity is increasingly rare. On the odd occasion when he does get some peace, the Doc's head is invariably screeching with the white noise of guilt and dissatisfaction and desperation. Sometimes, he just can't get away from himself, much as he would like to. But tonight he is resigned: resigned to giving up his day job once and for all – if he doesn't go, they'll push him anyway so he may as well; resigned to being exposed for his affair with Ellie and all the familial and professional consequences that that may have; resigned even to being put on some offender's register for dating an ex-student. Basically, this Doctor of English Literature has reached the point – and beyond – at which he just doesn't give a fuck. And, almost overnight, the white noise has disappeared.

But the cruel irony is that the trigger for this catharsis was a vicious row with Ellie. She had seemed sharp from the outset the previous night, after he'd called her late for a sneaky rendezvous on the Wednesday. They had been tetchy with one another the week before and now Ellie was not in the mood for sex. And the Doc was desperate for sex. And his wife was away so they could even go back to his place and take their time and be comfortable. But she didn't want it and she certainly would not have sex with him in his own conjugal bed. He was fuckin insensitive even to suggest it, apparently. So then came the usual machine-gun fire of inadequacies and infidelities and incompatibilities. Ellie unceremoniously ripped the Doc's life apart and made it clear that she was never going to be a part of its future. And where the Doc would normally revert, at this point, to the role of dough-eyed dreamer, he got very angry, partly because he had been denied a shag. The testosterone level rose very quickly and he rattled back with the linguistic equivalent of a Great War rifle. This extraordinarily erudite man simply couldn't find the words to express his frustrations and he just ended up accusing Ellie of taking his money and faking every orgasm she had had... or not had. It was less *Anthem for Doomed Youth* and more *Death Knell For A Sad Old Git*. After that, the evening went downhill fast and Ellie ended up walking back from Highcliffe Ridge – a good 2 miles – with the Doc kerb-crawling pathetically all the way to make sure she came to no harm, occasionally trying to reconcile their differences by dropping the passenger-side window and shouting 'I love you' over the sporadic whoosh of a late-night taxi.

So now he'd even fucked that one up n all. So who cares anymore? Nothing to lose at work, nothing to lose at home. Fuck it. May as well kick back and enjoy life without Nails for a few days – she's in Derbyshire seeing her sister, thank God. How could it get any worse?

He can hear Beany in the back. But he cannot see him and he's not within earshot. Beany's been grafting on his PhD lately and has been quite withdrawn: just coming in, doing his job and going home, with very little conversation. He's been worrying about Jonny too. The Doc can sense a nervousness around him but he's got too much on his plate to take on Beany's worries, what with everything else. It's all got a bit complicated with the Ellie thing and the Doc doesn't know how to approach it with Beany. He's kind of assuming that Mafe will take the strain on that front. And, at the moment, it does indeed feel like he is at the Front: hiding, ducking and diving, just surviving; but one day soon, he knows that he will have to go over the top and face what is coming to him.

The Doc takes the pint over to Mafe.

'I'll get the Dictionary – there's no way that's a word.'

Mafe doesn't even look up. He just waits for the pint to settle before taking a hearty swig, followed by a long sigh.

A few minutes pass. Tick tock tap. Tick tock tap. Tick tock tap. Mafe ponders the double-letter score above the word RUMINATE. Not a word of which he is particularly proud. Not a great score but a few minutes ago there seemed to be too many Rs floating about and he wanted rid. Mafe detests the letter R. He's never told anyone as much and there is no logic behind it but he would be quite happy without it. And now he's picked up another one and he is losing his patience. Mafe rarely loses his patience. Not even when he was asked to clear his desk at work, did he lose his patience. Not even when he was subpoenaed in front of the governors and indicted for almost every pedagogical crime in the vacuous *Guide to Modern Teaching Standards*, did he lose his patience. Not even when he was dressed down by a head of department half his age for deigning to take the side of a Newly Qualified Teacher in an argument over a parental complaint, did he lose his patience. Not even when the parent of the school's most abject pupil called him a fuckin waste o space who should just take himself into a corner and die quietly, did he lose his patience. Not even when he was fined by the private company which manages the new school building for parking in a visitor's spot, did he lose his patience. Mafe has endless patience.

But not quite. When the Board is going against him, when the letters are not slotting in neatly side by side, when the beautiful world of linguistic harmony seems to be turning on him in a fit of listless incongruity, well then Mafe loses his rag.

'What on earth are you doing, Mafe?'

'I'm trying to finish this bloody board. Only a handful of letters left in the bag. I'm really not in the mood tonight. Another bloody R. What am I supposed to do with that bloody thing? An F n all. Ridiculous.'

Mafe is at the bar. Not in Curmudgeon Corner. At the bar. But Mafe never sits up at the bar. Not by choice. He never even comes to collect his pint. And he most certainly doesn't move the hallowed board. Except on a Friday. When The Optic is full of drunks.

'That begins with an R, old boy.'

'What?'

'Ridiculous. It begins with a…'

'Don't need your help, twit. Any case, you looked up that lovely word marxize yet?' Mafe harrumphs.

'Yes. Two things about the word marxize: one, it is indeed a word; two, it relies quite heavily on the existence of the letter R. Without it, we'd have maxize and that would seem to me to be a likely Americanism used in a burger joint, or some such.'

The Doc thinks he's being clever.

'You do talk some absolute tosh, Doc. No wonder the kids give you grief.'

That's below the belt. Well below. That's disloyalty to the profession. A modern trait of teaching singularly responsible both for Mafe's early exit and for the Doc's present, unhappy predicament.

'Sorry, Doc. Out of order. Apologies. Not at all called for.'

'Never mind that, what the hell you at the bar for? Just to gloat over that lovely word containing both an X and a Z?'

'No, Doc. Not at all.'

And it is at this point that Mafe's face suddenly turns to alabaster. The Doc has not seen that face in years. Since he was last in the school building, in fact.

'Derek. Your car has been seen picking up a young student at Highcliffe Corner. Regularly, Derek. And I've come up here to let you know that people are going to…'

Beany is knelt under the bar sorting the lager glasses. Bit awkward really. Now he daren't stand upright. It'd be like standing proud on the Somme, he thinks, rather glibly. So that's three men in The Optic and two of them are now at the Front. The side door swings suddenly and violently through its hinges.

'There you are. Well isn't this nice n fuckin cosy? Just you n your old man, is it? Passin the time o day until you go out tonight n fuck another student, is it? Is the back o your car just as cosy is it? Or d'yer take 'er to a nice quiet spot in the trees, do yer? Fuck 'er as nature intended do yer? I can fuckin imagine, you dirty old twat – get yersen off in a couple o minutes n back to the fuckin missus is it? Or do yer bring 'er back 'ere even? Take 'er up the shitter on the fuckin conjugal fuckin sheets. Is that it? Nice n rude on the clean white sheets is it? I fuckin bet. N knowin your sort, you're probably filmin Jacques Cousteau-style n showing old Grandad ere, aren't yer? Give the old fucker a bit o pleasure before they start fuckin digging is 'ole, eh? Well I juss thought I'd pop in to say 'ello n to say I'm fuckin onto yer, old man. N when I find out oo the fuck you are, it'll be plastered on every fuckin lamp-post in the park before yer can get yer fuckin zip down n yer pathetic little cock out, yer dirty bastard.'

The door swings back through its hinges. Tick tock. Tick tock. Tick tock. Mafe stares at the letter F in his hand.

FERRUMINATE.

'That's not a word either.'

'I think you'll find that it is.'

The Doc opens the dictionary.

'Damn. Of course. This is volume 2. I need volume 1. One second.'

Mafe's left hand smothers the Doc's right.

'No. No. No. Composure, old boy. You already have volume 1 in hand – MARXIZE is M. And volume 2 begins N.'

'So you're right, Mafe.'

'I'm always right, Doc. Always.'

And in the end, Mafe *is* right – people are indeed going to find out.

Chapter 28

Jonny is shaking. Jonny often shakes. He shakes when he meets people he has not met before. He shakes when he thinks someone is about to ask him a question to which he does not know the answer. He shakes when he needs to clean his teeth and Saffi has not rinsed the sink after having a shave. But Jonny also shakes when he sees a familiar face in a crowd or on the street, he shakes when someone asks him a question to which he *does* know the answer. And he shakes when he peels the seal off a brand new tube of toothpaste and it comes away from the plastic aperture perfectly, without leaving any strands stuck to the rim. Tonight, Jonny is shaking in feverish desperation. And he is sweating. Profusely. And his cheeks are blood-red. They are blood-red because there is too much blood at the skin surface. They are the colour of blood because they are bloody. Because he is hot. And flustered. And vexed. And drugged.

When he comes into The Optic, Beany knows instantly that Jonny is hot. That he is flustered. That he is vexed. And that his cheeks are blood-red. But he doesn't suspect for one minute that Jonny has just taken an MDMA tablet and that he is in an overwhelming state of delirium. It would never occur to him that Jonny is coming up. But Jonny is coming up. He is coming right up. And when Beany asks Jonny if he is ok, Jonny starts giggling uncontrollably, cackling like a hyena and, as he loses control of his breath, he salivates rabidly and starts to spit and cough and choke. And Beany looks right into his eyes. And he sees the dilated pupils. And he sees the grinding jaw. And he watches as Jonny falls straight back off the barstool and onto the wooden floor. Jonny is coming up. And falling down. And now the floor is blood-red. And the back of Jonny's head is blood-red. And Beany's shaking hands are blood-red. And Beany panics. And Beany shouts to the Doc to call an ambulance and that he is going to get his mum and that Saffi is a fuckin dead man.

He runs. He runs and runs. And runs. And walks a hundred paces to calm his heartbeat and his anger. But the anger feeds the heartbeat and the heartbeat feeds the anger and he can't get there fast enough and he runs. He runs. He runs.

'What the fuck is wrong with Jonny? What the fuck av you bin doin to 'im now you little Paki prick? N where the fuck is M... Mum? Mum? Are you ok? What's the matter, Mum? What's that on your face? Why you sittin in the kitchen wi no clothes on? Where is ee? That fuckin bully boyfriend of yours? Mum, are you ok? Talk to me.'

The front door has buried itself into the inside wall and the kitchen door swings open and shut again before Beany realises that there's only Mum. Mum is alone, cowed, crying. Blood again. Head in hands, she's slumped forward on an old wooden canteen chair, bowed like a half-time footballer being told he's shite. Agate, agog, aghast at her own pathetic existence. Beany panics. Again. He doesn't ask. He scoops her up in her dressing gown and puts her in the car. And drives. And drives. And drives. Mum's car bleeps at him. 'Fuckoff, I know I'm not wearing a fuckin seatbelt. Fucksake.' And he drives. Straight through red. Straight over roundabouts. Straight down the one way. Straight into the AnE car park.

'Yes. Marion Hainsworth. 26.02.52. Yes. No. I don't know. Head injury. Yes. Mum, have you been asleep? No, no she hasn't. What? No, I wasn't with her when... No. Mum, have you eaten recently? Mum? Mum, have you eaten anything? Yes, yes I think probably yes... there were dirty pots in the kitchen... assume she has... yes. Ok. Yes, right, yes, ok.'

They sit. They wait. They watch. Screaming mothers. Screaming kids. Angry dads. Angry drunks. Crying loved ones. Raw bones and joints. Raw hatred. Liquid pouring out of every vein and orifice. Red and yellow and brown in all directions. Phones buzzing and bleeping and whining and vibrating. People buzzing and bleeping and whining and vibrating. Staff almost staying calm and forcefully declining to tolerate verbal fuckin abuse. Oh for fucksake he's been here nearly 3 hours and his dad's home alone and he can't get up the stairs. Oh for fucksake she's been here more than 4 and there are people in fuckin Ethiopia getting better treatment than her. Oh for fucksake if ee sez I fuckin touched 'im I'll fuckin kill 'im cos I never n he wo slagging off mi bird n eez such a fuckin gobshite n I got this tryin to 'elp 'im the fucker. It only needs a couple o stitches n I told you I lost my fuckin wallet...

'Mr Hainsworth? Come this way, please. No, your mum can stay seated. Just need to talk to you.'

'Oh, ok, yes, yes, yes I do. Yes, Jonny. Yes, he fell off a barstool at the local pub. The bloke with him is no relation. He's the landlord of the pub. Yes, ok, yes. Is he ok? Yes, what do you mean? Yes, he's a really good bloke. He's a teacher at the local school. Sorry? What? Well where is he then? What, me? No. How would I know? I didn't come in with them. No, my mother. Yes. No she wasn't in the pub. No. At home.'

Beany sits down again. Mum has started lolling into somnolence.

'Mum. Mum. You can't sleep. Don't sleep, Mum. Sit up. Mum, please sit up. It won't be long.'

And it isn't. It isn't long at all. It isn't long before a policeman comes and takes them to a side room. It isn't long before Beany is told that his mum has no injuries. That the blood on her hands and face and clothes is not hers. That a nosy neighbour had heard screams and shouts and gone into her house, whose front door had been left buried in the interior wall. That he had found nobody in downstairs. That he had gone upstairs and found the body of an Asian man, aged around 50, naked, with two lacerations in his neck and semen on his midriff. That there was blood all over the bedroom floor. And it isn't long before he is told that the man who brought his brother in had checked him in, then disappeared. That his brother is being treated for the suspected effects of Ecstasy. That they need to contact the man who brought him in to establish the circumstances of his accident and the exact nature of his ingestions.

And now there is so much black in Beany's head that the whitened walls and the whitened coats and the whitened faces around him are too close and too bright and too unnerving. And he doesn't remember much after that. In fact, he doesn't remember anything after that.

Chapter 29

The hum of rubber on tarmac, molten from a day in the near-equatorial heat, is soporific. The Doc is lethargic. He sits at Jonny's feet, not really thinking about anything, vague images of unmarked exercise books, settling pints and Ellie's naked, nubile body in the forest leaves wandering in and out of his consciousness.

The paramedic would – and quite possibly should – be talking to Jonny about Jonny, to make sure he doesn't fall asleep and to establish some basic facts before they arrive at hospital. But Jonny doesn't let him get a word in. He is telling Roger about his girlfriend. About how he met her at University. About how beautiful she is. About her Dr. Martens and her physical and intellectual awkwardness. About her fantastic taste in music and her longing to be a writer and about how he walks her home most nights. About how they haven't had sex yet because she wants to wait until they are married and he hopes she wants a big family because he wants lots of kids and he is hoping that he can get a good job so that she will not have to work. And about how she has lots of other men fancying her but that she was the one who approached him and helped him to find some books for his University work. About how he doesn't understand what she sees in him and that he is just so lucky to have her.

Strangely, he doesn't mention her name. He doesn't mention that she was one of the Doc's students, that she is studying English and Philosophy, that she works in the University library. He doesn't mention that she regards him as a stalker and a pervert. He doesn't mention that she has told him to fuck right off on numerous occasions. He doesn't mention that he has followed her home countless times. He doesn't mention that he has also followed her to her dealer's house and seen them smoking weed and having sex. And he doesn't mention that she then goes to meet Dr Ramsbottom at Highcliffe Corner and that he has told Dr Ramsbottom of her sexual deviances.

He doesn't mention any of this. Until the MDMA starts to wear off. And he starts coming down. And an overwhelming lucidity takes hold. It's like someone has dissected his brain with a scalpel and turned each half inside out, perfectly reflecting all that is inside. Except that the real image is the not a reflection but a refraction of the virtual image. The truth will out.

'Ellie. What a lovely name, Jonny. Is it short for Eleanor, Jonny?'

'Yes. Yes it is.'

Jonny is crying now.

'No it isn't. It isn't Eleanor at all. It's Eliana. And were Mr Hainsworth to know her as he purports, he would know that.'

Roger the paramedic looks at the Doc.

'Sorry, Mr errr Dr Ramsbottom. We just need to keep him talking and as lucid as possible. Can we try and keep this on a level, please?'

The Doc has no idea what 'on a level' means.

'Oh, yes. Yes, of course. Sorry. How very insensitive of me. Sorry.'

The ambulance docks in AnE. Doors open, stretchers click and clack. A blast of night air. Roger jumps down and out and disappears briefly down the side of the ambulance. And Jonny is left exposed.

Roger is down and out and Jonny is exposed. The Doc is both.

Chapter 30

Beany has to take Jonny to his student house, the officer says. Just for the time being, the officer says. Just until the Ecstasy in Jonny's system has worn off, the officer says. Just until Jonny has calmed down, the officer says. Just until he falls asleep, the officer says. Just to give everyone time to come up for air, the officer says. Just until the police can lock down Mum's house and establish what has happened, the officer says. Just until Mum has seen a counsellor and been interviewed with a lawyer, the officer says. Just until they need to speak to him again. And Jonny. The officer says.

The officer walks Jonny and Beany to the hospital exit. Beany says thank you very much and starts walking. He can't remember which car park he's in. He holds Jonny's hand. He hasn't held Jonny's hand for years. He worries that Jonny will pull away, reject him. He worries that if Jonny does pull away, he won't have the strength to stay upright. And that he'll fall. Unbroken. Flat on his face. Broken. But Jonny holds on tight. Jonny is shaking again. Jonny is coming down. And he seems to have come down so far that he is now below the point he was at when he started coming up. Beany sees graphs and wavy lines in his head. Up, up, up, going up. Then down, down, further down, down below the axis line. Into the Red. Whatever that is. Out of control, lost it. Fuck, he's losin the plot.

He's probably right. He probably is losing the plot. Beany has spent the last hour nodding at everyone who has said something to him. The words coming out of their mouths have just been words. Isolated, unconnected, meaningless words.

Randomly organised letters randomly juxtaposed with other randomly organised letters to make up randomly organised sentences. With no sense. So, not really sentences, then. And all Beany sees is Grandad in Curmudgeon Corner, flailing and fraying, as pint after pint of No 3 is poured all over his Scrabble board, the letters swimming frantically to recover some semblance of meaning. Some clinging on to their brethren and with them a desperate coherence. Others cascading hopelessly onto the wooden floor and losing all cogency and significance, slow-drowned in alcoholic isolation. And now the board has been tossed up into the air. And Grandad is shouting and crying and railing uncontrollably. They should never have fuckin pushed me, he says, the bastards all stabbed me in the back just because I wouldn't be complicit in the duplicity and the plagiarism and the open cheating and the results-fixing. Fuckin moribunds, the fuckin lot of them, I'll fuckin gouge their eyes out if I ever fuckin set eyes on the bastards again. And Beany knows it cannot be Grandad because Grandad just doesn't talk like that and he doesn't use words in that way and some of those words he would never use at all. And, in any case, he wouldn't react like that. He'd pick up the board and dry out all the pieces and get back to his game. Re-establish the order and the primacy of the lexicon. That's what he'd do. Sure as Beany is holding Jonny's hand right now. It cannot be Grandad. But Beany cannot see the face and he cannot see who it is. And, worse, he cannot see the face of the pint-pourers or the board-bashers or the spineless bastards who are treating Grandad in this way. He cannot see their faces because they have no face. They are the faceless ones. The ones who have spent years undermining and underhanding. The ones who have spent years backstabbing and backhanding. The ones who have spent years disarming and dismantling. The ones who have spent years denying and denigrating. The ones who have spent years killing knowledge and killing curiosity. The carefree, the careless. The cunts.

Oh, yes, Beany is most definitely losing the plot. Of course he is. He must be. Just like Grandad. Except that, Beany isn't losing the plot. He isn't losing the plot at all. He thinks he is. He walks like he is. All military and straight-line and stupid. He talks like he is. All brawn and babel and babble. But he isn't. He can't be. There is no plot to lose. Least, none that he knows about. Mum killed Saffi in self-defence. He was a first-rate bastard. He deserved it. No plot. Nothing to understand. Mum should be home by teatime, as she always is.

Beany looks round at Jonny. Jonny is sniffling like a baby. He is virtually sleepwalking. He is holding out a handful of sealy bags. Beany snatches them and holds them up to a streetlight – ecstasy and whizz. For sure.

'Who the fuck gave you these, Jonny? Who gave you these drugs?'

'Pete did. Pete did, Sean. You must know Pete. You must. Everyone seems to know Pete. Pete is a very famous man. And Pete is a very lucky man. Very, very lucky. He has no idea how lucky he bloody well is.'

'Jonny.'

Beany turns to face Jonny and stops him in his tracks, shaking him, shaking him quite hard.

'Jonny. What the fuck are you talking about? Who is Pete? Why did he give you these drugs? What does he want from you? Do you owe him money or something? Are you selling them for him? What the fuck is going on, Jonny? Is this bloke fucking with you?'

'The only person Pete is fucking is Ellie, Sean. Ellie Barakowski. My beautiful Ellie.'

'Jonny, fucksake. Where is this guy? Where does he live? Do you know?'

'Yes of course I know. I follow Ellie to his house every Thursday night. She goes in, they fuck, they smoke weed, and then she walks to meet her dad. Who is actually Dr Ramsbottom.'

'What? What the fu… Jonny, do you know the address?'

'Yes of course I know. I just told you. I'll take you there if you want. It's easy. It'll only take ten minutes from here.'

But Jonny needs to be inside. Jonny needs to be safe. Jonny needs to be looked after. Beany knows that. He is wavering in and out of conscious thought. He is talking nonsense. He is not making any sense. He is undoubtedly making things up. And he is still under the influence of the drugs he has taken. And in any case, the officer says he needs to be home. And safe. And not alone.

But Beany needs to find this bastard dealer.

'Where, Jonny, where?'

'117 Carsley Crescent.'

So he leaves Jonny with Gareth. Gareth looks vexed. He doesn't look happy at all. He looks like his whole evening has been ruined. He looks like he's about to chin Beany. But he doesn't know all that has just happened and Beany doesn't have time to explain and could he just please take care of Jonny for a little while... please? And Beany doesn't wait for an answer and shuts the front door on the two of them before Gareth can do anything.

Chapter 31

Jonny stares at the plate on the square, pine kitchen table. The plate is oval, off-white and the base is set slightly deeper, creating a ridge between that and the outer. Jonny imagines it having been made in two pieces and stuck together. Gareth's mouth is moving very aggressively but Jonny is just trying to work out what the plate had on it before the meal was consumed. There's a greeny liquid swimming around a more viscous yellow substance and quite coarse white particles are buoyed in the meniscus. Fried eggs. But what's the green and where's the brown sauce residue? Everyone has brown sauce on eggs. You have to have brown sauce on eggs.

The toilet is flushed upstairs. Bare feet pad the boards and a door squeaks on its hinges. A bed mattress sighs. A mobile buzzes.

The table is arranged like a memory game, like a nutritional and existential microcosm of student life – lighter, random keys, coinage adding up to next to nothing, earphones, ingrained mugs – one used as an ashtray, a gaping pizza box, a partially torn newspaper, all dusted and scattered with flakes of tobacco, marijuana crumbs and discarded roaches. And a copy of Dostoevsky's *Crime and Punishment*. The spine is warped and the pages are jaundiced at the edges. But it doesn't look conscientiously thumbed. It looks like it's been there for months, maybe even years, handed down from one student household to another as a token of intellectualism. Someone has scrawled his name on the inside cover, with a date. February 1976.

'Who is James Peterson?'

Gareth stops ranting for a second.

'What? Who? No bloody idea, Jonny. Have you not been listening to a word I've said?'

'But his name is in this book and it is on the table and you have obviously just eaten so I assume you are reading it. Did James Peterson give you this book, in which case you must know who he is?'

'What? Jesus, Jonny. It's not even my book. Why do you assume it's mine just because it's on the kitchen table? It isn't. I've never read a word of it. I don't even know what it is. It just sits there and no one ever seems to take it or read it or use it for anything.'

'What's the green?'

Gareth is agitated. He cannot be here. He simply cannot be here. He has to go out. He has to meet someone soon and he can't stay in much longer. He has stuff to do.

'And how come there are two plates and who is the girl in your room, Gareth?'

'What? What the f? What girl? What about the green? It's asparagus, Jonny. You never had asparagus, Jonny?'

'Who's the girl, Gareth? N why did you tell Ellie your name was Sean and is it Ellie upstairs, Gareth?'

'Are you hungry, Jonny? I've just cooked poached eggs with asparagus and a hollandaise sauce. It was lovely. If you're hungry, I'll happily make you some.'

'Thought you were in a rush to go out, Gareth?'

'I... I... I am, I need to be somewhere but Beany is a mate and I said I'd look after you so how about those poached eggs? You do look as though you could do with some sustenance, Jonnyboy.'

Jonny hates it when Gareth calls him Jonnyboy. It makes him sound like a backward farmer's boy. Jonny hates it when he is made to feel thick. And in any case, he's never lived on a farm and why would he want to? And he's sure there are farmer's boys who are not thick. But he is hungry. He is very hungry. He's heard Sean and his friends call it the munchies.

Drugs make you mad and then tired and then very, very hungry. And Jonny is very, very hungry. And besides, he has things he needs to say to Gareth and he doesn't want him to go out and leave him.

'Yes. Please.'

'What do you want? Eggs? Bacon? Sausage? Think Beany might have some Fulton's burgers in the freezer. They're shit but they'll fill a hole…'

Gareth is rifling and scurrying. Looking for anything to feed Jonny and move the conversation on.

'You study Food Science. Don't you, Gareth?'

'Yes, why? What do you want to eat?'

'Well then you must be a very good chef, I reckon.'

'Not sure about that but I can always put something edible on a plate, Jonny. Tell me what you want.'

'Do you have brown sauce? You have to have brown sauce with eggs, don't you, Gareth?'

'Yes I do indeed. Eggs n brown sauce, then?'

'What is asparagus, Gareth?'

'What? You don't know what asparagus is?'

'No. I don't think my mum cooks it and, in any case, Saffi's always cooking curry and you can't even see what's in a curry, can you Gareth?'

'You can in a good one, Jonny. Maybe I'll make you one sometime.'

'You lie all the time, don't you Gareth? To get what you want, I mean? You tell people things that aren't true, don't you? Just to get them to do what you want them to do.'

Gareth has to go out. He has to. It's Thursday. It's drugs night and one, he's all out of weed, two, he's on a night tomorrow and he needs some tabs and, three, he has to catch Ellie when she gets to Pete's. He needs to find out if he's been rumbled.

'You told Ellie your name is Sean. Why did you do that? Why did you deceive that lovely girl and use my brother's name to get her into your car and probably your bed? Why did you do that, Gareth?'

Gareth really needs to get out. But he's being interrogated. Interrogated by Detective Inspector Autism. Who notices everything. Who remembers everything. Who analyses everything. Whose interpretation of everything is black and white, right or wrong, good or bad. And once he's decided it's black, or wrong, or bad, then it is. It is black. It is wrong. It is bad. And that makes Gareth black, and wrong, and bad.

Gareth fires up the hob and melts some butter in a pan. Silence and brown sauce are his only possible defence now. He pulls up the sash to let in the warm evening air. There's rain around and a dampness. But the stagnant humidity of the afternoon remains. And these post-Victorian terraces, with their thick walls and minimal ventilation, get stuffy. And Gareth feels the claustrophobia. Of the weather. Of the guilt. Of Jonny's exocet line of questioning.

Music. Instrumental, post-rock, jazz-infused, post-apocalypse. An air of suspense, of emotive poignancy, of threat. Musicman is in pensive mood tonight. And he cannot realise how beautifully he has caught the mood across the road. Jonny smells onions and garlic and the acridity of peppers. The bitterness is unmistakeable. As is the music. At least to Jonny.

'Do Make Say Think.'

'Sorry?' Gareth leans over the sink to fill the kettle without turning round.

'The music. I've got this CD. It's brilliant. They're a Canadian band from the same musical circles as Godspeed You Black Emperor! It's psychedelic, it's dub, it's lounge, it's electronica, it's visceral. It's one of my favourite albums.'

Gareth ignores the unlikely erudition but not the musical gambit. A chance to deviate.

'I saw Godspeed at Bradford St George's Hall a few years ago. There must have been 30 of them on the stage. It was fabulous but they really ought to have seated everyone. They're an orchestra. The venue was perfect but we were all standing there gently swaying for 2 hours. An orchestra needs an orchestral venue. Don't you think?'

'I'd love to have seen them. They're one of my favourite bands. Ellie loves them, you know.'

Just as Gareth thinks he might have taken the conversation onto safer territory. Boom. Another grenade is unclipped.

A phone buzzes upstairs. A creak of bedstead, feet padding. Shoes click-clack. Door whines open. Jonny counts the stairs as she comes down heavily. So does Gareth. He chops the garlic nice n fine. 14 clomps. And the noise of her gladbag on the stairwell wall like a cheese grater. She appears at the kitchen door. Blonde bob, tits, slim, heels, scouse.

'I'm goin, Gaz. Thanks for the food. It was lovely. I'll see yer later.'

She doesn't wait for an acknowledgment. Or to be introduced to Jonny. She just goes. Easy in. Easy out. She probably has a name. She probably has a lovely personality. She probably enjoys good food and good company and good sex and good drugs. And she definitely does know Gareth's name. Unlike Ellie.

'Ellie is fuckin Pete, yer know. Your dealer has been shagging her every time she goes round for her weed. I see them. Every Thursday. She'll do anything with 'im, yer know. She sucks 'im off, she turns on all fours while ee wanks all over her, he fucks 'er up the arse as 'ard as ee can. She just seems to accept it as part of the deal. Or maybe she loves 'im. Maybe she is madly in love with 'im.'

The garlic starts to burn ever so slightly. The music crescendos bass, percussion and ethereal guitar.

'Maybe it's 'is huge dick. Maybe she just likes a little bit of pain with her sex. N you know what is really impressive? Really impressive?' …

A flick of the grill for the toast. Tears flecked across his eyes. Nothing to say.

… 'She goes straight from there to meet the Doc. Dr Ramsbottom. At Highcliffe Corner. And they often drive out to the edge of the woods and have very quick, shitty sex in the back of his car. And I bet ee talks literature with her and she fawns over his outstanding mind.'

'Fucksake. Why doesn't anyone ever clean the fuckin grill after they've used it? How am I supposed to do toast now? Fucksake.'

'So, basically. She goes from one huge dick to one huge brain. She gets it all in one evening. As well as some lovely drugs and a ride in a warm car.'

Gareth unhooks the asparagus from above the sink and starts to tip them, drawing rather than lifting the knife with that smooth technique only chefs seem to have.

'So what the hell she would want with you, Mr Simpson (or is it Hainsworth?), I don't know. I really do not know.'

'Now the eggs are gonna be done and the toast will be late. Bloody Hainsworth again.'

'I'll give you one thing, mind. Ghostpoet. Now that was a good choice. I think Pete approved n all. Think ee likes a bit of urban poetry. Maybe ee just loves the lazy delivery of a crucial lyric. Like I do. Maybe we are all more alike than we pretend. Maybe that's why we all want to fuck Ellie. She's delicious, don't you think?'

Gareth is lurching and lunging around the kitchen, exasperated.

'Talkin of which. Don't you need to put the asparagus on before the eggs?'

Gareth stops dead over the table. He looks at the mess. He looks back out the window to the source of the music, which has now become invasive, irritating. And he looks at Jonny. He stares but does not see. He hesitates and yet his decision is made.

'Does Ellie let you have anal sex with her, Gareth? Or is that what the titty scouser was about?'

And right on the word 'titty', the front door clicks shut behind him. And Gareth is gone.

Jonny sits for a while. He's not sure how long. And then he cannot bear it any longer. He gets up sharply, scraping the chair on the wooden floor, and starts to do the washing up. The eggs have disintegrated into the boiling water. The asparagus is still on the chopping board. And the grill is busy burning the remnants of last night's sausages.

Chapter 32

'D' yer want another No 3, Mafe?'

'Beg your pardon, dear?'

'No 3?' She holds up three fingers. Painted. Polished. Bejewelled. Gloriously Gucci.

He shivers. 'Oh, yes, right, yes please, that would be splendid. Since it's a special occasion. I will.'

She doesn't ask. Unlikely. The wife is no more than bones and formicary and the nearest blood relative is the shep asleep at his feet. It's been a good while since Mr Mayfield had a 'special occasion'.

'QUIXOTIC. That's 26 plus 20 for a triple letter score on Q. 46. Very pleasing.'

He does that thing again. He always tugs at the sleeves of his cardy when he's scored heavily. Must be a good game because there are new holes appearing in the forearm. Maybe that's the occasion – a record Scrabble score.

Nails brings over the pint.

'That bloody cardy's on its last legs, Mafe. I'll 'ave to get you a new one for yer birthday.'

'Not necessary, dear. I doubt I'll make another birthday and, in any case, I'm rather attached to this old thing.'

'Nonsense. You're a creaking gate, old lad. You'll go on longer than me.'

Mafe doesn't hear. Now that a fresh pint is settling, he's gone back into the world of words. Nails takes a good, long look at him. She does love him, silly old fruitcake that he is. The cardigan is indeed threadbare and it's even worse close-up. Still, the tie affords him some dignity. Well, it would if it didn't have an impromptu beer and crisps look about it. It used to be mauve. Whatever that is. The undergrads would laugh at him when he used words like 'mauve'. He never did quite work out at what precise point the lexical lothario becomes the listless leech.

'Oh for heaven's sake. Another Q. What is a man to do with a U-less Q?'

'Better than a clueless you.' The voice comes from the cellar.

There is someone hovering over him now. It almost seems that the pale, pasty pout looking straight at him has retorted without moving her lips. But Old Mafe sees the vacuity in this hunched shell. She didn't say it. She doesn't have the wit, the intelligence, the linguistic guile. And the countenance is that of an undercooked pie parched of its gravy. She is microwave food. Physically and intellectually. He thinks of his wife – just the observation she'd have spat out loud. God, he misses her. Mealy-mouthed, monotone, moribund, he thinks. Not his beloved, this woman standing over him.

'Now then… MORIBUND…' He's looking at an M and an O. 'If I can pick up a B, there's a link on a word ending D. Not a bad score just to keep me tick… Arggh, another bloody R. That letter'll be the death of me…'

'Ok to park myself here?'

'Sorry? I beg your pardon?'

'Is anyone sitting here?'

'No, no, not at all. No one ever dares sit adjacent to an old snorter like me.'

'Are you winning?'

'Huh. You entirely miss the point, dear girl.' She's riled him already. Sharp intake of breath. Mafe straightens himself.

'On this 12 inch square board in this back-alley drinking den barely a stone's throw from the condescending cosmotropolis, nature and nurture are ever so tightly woven as the tapestry of life. Beautiful words so lovingly crafted, thousands of immaculate conceptions emanating from who knows where. Every eve the letters tell a different story – they allude, they etch, they release. As the green baize bag is emptied, a whole world opens up to us. It's like a semantic Pandora's Box. This is the great tapestry of life. Here. All on this little cardboard square. Every time I pick out another letter, a new world is born. A new life. It puts breath in my lungs and marrow in my bones, dear girl. And all washed down with a germinal gallon of Younger's finest. This is no race, my dear. There is nothing to be won. Words are like love, my dear. Intangible, unprized, quixotic.' He chuckles.

'Younger's? Did you say Younger's?'

'Yes indeed. Been drinking it for as long as I've had a sheppie and she's my fourth.' The dog barely stirs.

'Funny that. My dad was a taster for Younger's most of his working life. Put out to grass, he was. When it closed. So who's brewing that? An old witch in the attic?'

'There's a taxi for you outside.' Nails has come over.

'I haven't ordered a taxi.'

'I know. I have. On your behalf. Thank you.'

'Excuse me?'

'Derek. This lady is just leaving.'

'Very well.'

The voice echoes but gets closer. He's just coming up from the cellar.

'Oh, it's you. What are you doing in here? You never come in here?'

'I know. I came in looking for you and got talking to this old fella.'

'Well, you're not welcome. Taxi is waiting. And why would you want me?'

'But I've just bought a GnT and I'm comfortable.'

'Yes. But I'm not. And neither is Mr Mayfield.'

'How does he know? He's so batty he thinks he's drinking a beer that's not been brewed for 20 years.'

'Enough. I'm the landlord and in here we don't re-write other people's history. They have the freedom to write their own. So save your bastardisations for the next Maths GCSE you'll no doubt be re-writing for another batch of poor, unassuming little shits. Goodnight.'

She is gone. The witch is away on her broom. The witch's brew is still clinging triumphantly to Mafe's glass. The Doc comes back inside.

'She get safely into the cab, D?'

'No, Mafe, she didn't.'

'Who was sh… sorry? She didn't? Oh? Should someone not be attending…?'

'No, Mafe. There was no taxi. Now enjoy your pint… oh and… you have got a U there and you've also got a BLANK under your sleeve, you silly old git… QUORUM down there on a triple letter score on Q… that's 37, old boy.'

'Damn. Why the Devil did I not see that?'

And then the Doc does something he has never done before. Never. The Doc sits down. Slightly intimately. And Mafe is unnerved. The Doc never sits down. He never gets involved in the Scrabble at close quarters. He would rather lean over Mafe's shoulder and interject with an annoyingly good and obvious word every now and then, or glance at the board in passing and slink off into his study to peruse the OED, before coming back triumphant, as though to prove his intellectual worth after another demoralising day in the classroom, or simply to humour Mafe for a few seconds. But now he is studying the board, considering the letters in Mafe's hand and suggesting possibilities. And then, particularly irksome, whispering the score calculations to himself, incoherently. And he sits there for a full half-hour. He doesn't engage in any conversation, he doesn't even ask after Mafe's dog, which is busy licking the Doc's shoes under the table. Probably the blood and the disinfectant. The Doc unfailingly asks about the dog. And his interest has always seemed genuine. But he doesn't mention it at all. He just sits and comes out with word after word after word. And Mafe is too astounded at the erudition and the sheer quantity of words pouring out of the Doc's mouth to ask him what on earth he is doing. He just knows something is not right. And the Doc doesn't mention

182

Jonny. He doesn't explain that Jonny came in earlier, clearly unwell and under the influence of something. That he'd promptly fallen backwards off a barstool, cracked his head and been ambulanced to hospital. That, in the course of the ambulance journey, Jonny had gone on a very obtuse mental rant in which he unravelled the fatuousness and the deceit of the Doc's entire existence.

A mouthful of words and Mafe is speechless, uncomfortable. And yet they have always been his salvation. Well, nearly always. Except when he tried to explain to the board of governors why results had slipped from 68 to 66 per cent. Another gobful and the Doc's life has been arrested, tried and sentenced, hung, drawn and quartered, bagged, packed and sealed, cleaned, embalmed and buried. Bang. Dead. Dig the hole. Hammer in the nails. All over. One-nil. Fucked. And the Doc is sitting right next to Mafe now, feeling the soil falling over his head.

The Doc doesn't mention any of this. Because it would mean him explaining why he hadn't taken Jonny in his car, not to mention justifying his entire life and confessing to The Cardinal Sin in front of his wife. The irony is that the Doc doesn't really care anymore. And he is pretty sure that Nails wouldn't give a shit either, as long as the money were shared nice and calmly between them, thus leaving him morally and literally bankrupt, destitute. Come to think of it, that's not the irony. The irony is that he has come back from the hospital – via a couple of short, sharp cognacs in a shady bar in town – with the express intention of standing Nails up in the bar, looking her straight in the over-pencilled eyes and telling her that he is fucking a 21 year old student with a tight fanny and pert tits. And if half the fuckin nosy neighbourhood happen to be in the bar for a good drink at that point, all the better. All the more hilarious. All the more outstandingly appropriate, to use Wilhelm's stupid, vacuous word. So he has come home all warm and jaunty and cheerful and offered to go straight down to do the evening cellar check. And Nails thinks it's weird because she knows he hates that job. Of all the jobs. The spidery, web-sticky pumps, the awkward, barrel-shaped barrels, the piss-poor light, the smell of stale hops and rat urine, the dank, and the simple manualism of it all. But he has seen the paucity of the audience and decided that he might wait for a bit of a gathering before springing out of the cellar and landing his blows on Nails' ugly mug. And then she has appeared. Of all people. Mrs fuckin Appropriate. Mrs fuckin Might We Just Have A Quiet Word fuckin Appropriate. Never has she set fuckin foot in his sanctuary before. Never. She wouldn't dare. Fine, during the day, he almost accepts that he is in for some slow, asperous torture. And that it will only get more painful. And that she will steadily grind him down. Chip away, chip, chip away, day after fuckin day after fuckin day after fuckin day. Until he crumbles and tells her to fuck off or takes a baseball bat to her philistine head or just walks out the building in the middle of the worst bottom set he's ever clapped eyes on. Or some fuckin thing. But not here. Not in The Optic. Not in the only place in the world where they cannot get to him. And now, she has got to him. Just by being here. Just by turning up. And he feels exposed, shamed, bereft. And he hasn't even told her. He hasn't even tried. He cannot find the words. Oh yes, he can find any word in the OED to champion Mafe's stupid fuckin board of lexical nonsense. He can find BRIGUE and CONDIGNITY and FLAX and ISCHIUM and KREEF. But he cannot find the combination to say look, I'm human and I fell for this student and she is beautiful and sexy and flighty and exciting and she makes me feel alive again and I am in love with her and I'm sorry and I know this is wrong and awful and devastating to the lovely life of tranquillity we had planned and I never meant to hurt you but in the end I am in love with her and for as long as I am we have no future and I cannot live this dishonest existence any longer I'm really sorry I really truly am... He cannot do it. Just like he cannot turn to Mafe and say I'm really sorry I completely neglected to tell you that Jonny was in here earlier and I didn't want to frighten you because he's fine now but he fell off a barstool and hit his head and he needed stitches and I took him to hospital and he's fine and...

actually I didn't take him to hospital, technically, but the ambulance did because I knew he'd recognise my car and actually I didn't wait around to see him home safe because he told me he knew about my seeing Ellie and I panicked and I went AWOL and drank a couple of whiskies and, no, I don't actually know where he is now but I promise he's fine and, well, maybe he isn't because it seems he'd taken some drugs and, no, I don't know where Sean is and… shit… And now he despises Mafe – lovely, kind, uplifting Mafe, the man who represents everything about education that he holds dear and who is his only remaining link to a beautiful past of learning for learning's sake – because Mafe is only interested in words. And, right now, they are no fuckin use to him. No fuckin use at all. That's the irony. That's the fucked-up irony.

'D, can you come sort these glasses out, love? Since we're quiet we might as well dust down this end of the bar. I didn't think, exams are all finishing now and they'll all be going home, won't they?'

The Doc hovers. He stands. He takes one step towards the bar. Nope. No words.

'Sorry, love. I just need to go out for a bit. I feel like shit.'

Chapter 33

The military, sagittal stomp of Sean Hainsworth is now taking him straight round to number 117 Carsley Crescent. To the house where a bloke called Pete lives.

'Fuck me, another weirdo on the doorstep. Who the fuck are you? Let me guess, you're either a fuckin snout or another meth addict who can't read the fuckin words LATE NIGHT PHARMACY.'

Pause. Beany stares straight into the heavily-dilated pupils of Pete Verity.

'My name is Sean Hainsworth. You must be Pete. The infamous Pete. The man who is so famous he is known only by his first name. Pete.'

Beany's enunciation feeds heartily on the fricatives, emphasising in heavy irony the importance of this man they call, simply, Pete.

'Fuck me, how many fuckin Sean fuckin Hainsworths are there, for fucksake?'

'Well since you ask, just the one in my world.'

'Oh yes, of course, it's all getting a bit fuckin clearer now. I must try some o these pills again. They're fuckin champion, these. I'm seein things I ain't never seen before, fucksake. You're Jonny's brother, aren't you, old son? Well fuck me if I 'aven't met the whole family in one evening. A pleasure, old twat. Please do come the fuck in.'

Beany stands at the threshold. He stares. He has not flinched since Pete started talking. Beany has no intention of going in. He has the feeling that a few pregnant pauses will elicit quite a bit of information here without him saying a word, albeit couched sharply in f words, c words and possibly most other expletives.

'Tell me, Mr Hainsworth, did Jonny enjoy his little trip earlier?'

Silence. Rustling leaves in the gathering breeze.

'I mean, the first E is always the best. He must 'av bin fuckin bangin like a shithouse door in a storm within an hour or so, eh?'

Silence. Beany feels a drop or two of rain in the air.

'See, Mr Hainsworth, you're quite interestin to me. And there aren't many people oo really interest me. It's more their 'abits, knowhatameanlike?'

He draws his head in a lateral movement and a virtual line of coke up his nose.

'You see, Mr Hainsworth. I bin sellin a bit o gear to a Sean 'ainsworth for quite a few months now an, well, eez always paid up sharp, like. 'Cept once. N once is once too often for me. I'm a businessman, see. There's rules. There's deadlines, see. Well, ee missed one. N I came a knockin. Ee weren't in. Which, at the time, concerned me a little. 'Is safety, you understand? Anyway, ee settled pretty bloody quickly when my lads caught up wi 'im n it were all fine. Funny thing is, though. I'm sure it were you I talked to when I came round. I don't forget a face, Mr 'ainsworth.'

He leans right into Sean's face.

'Never.'

'N neither do I, Mr Pete. Neither do I.'

Beany leans right into Pete's eyeline.

'You are indeed correct, Mr Pete. It was indeed me you saw that evening. N it's good to meet you again, finally. Because my ID to the police that eve was a little sketchy on account of you havin come at the house from a slightly, shall we say, unusual angle and then disappearin in an equally unorthodox way. But now I'm getting a very nice look at you. N the ID later tonight shouldn't be too much of a problem.'

Pete lunges and takes hold of Beany's throat. He has a deceptively strong wrist and Beany can't easily loosen his grip. It's raining. Steadily. And Beany is getting wet. Very. So he does the logical thing. He reacts the way many lads would, be it instinct or the influence of TV: Beany punches Pete clean on the left jaw.

There is a moment of vacuum. No voice, no air, no movement. And then Pete's hand detaches from Beany's neck. And he falls backwards onto the entrance stairwell. The back of his head hits the bottom step hard. The shock, the back spasm and the drugs put paid to a rebound. He just stares up at Beany. No one does that to Pete Verity. No one. Except that someone just has. And Beany stands over Mr Pete to ensure that Mr Pete gets the message. And to shelter from the downpour, just for a second or two.

'One, don't ever come near my brother again. Two, I have the drugs you sold to him and the police will have them within the hour. And three, the fella I think you were referring to before was Mr Gareth Simpson. And he happens to be a very good friend of mine. Whatever debt he may have, or had, to you is hereby settled. Capiche?'

Beany does not wait for an answer. He's quite wet enough now. And he's shaking. He wouldn't have got one anyway. At least, not a verbal one.

Chapter 34

Highcliffe Grill is a classy joint. Formica, woodchip and all-day breakfasts for less than a fiver. The students used to come here in their droves but there's no wi-fi and there are burgers to be had and the fat bird behind the counter is just not luvvin it at all. So it's mostly waifs and strays and leftovers from the banquet of student life – discarded locals, halls of residence cleaners and failed grads who never grew up. At least there are no parking issues and mobiles are not forever binging and ringing and trilling.

The people who wander in here come to do one of two things: pass the time of day or watch. The pass-the-timers are seldom watchers. They are grannies with thick glasses and few teeth and plastic shopping trolleys on two wheels. There never seems to be anything in the trolleys. They talk about grandchildren and haemorrhoids and they make the cup of tasteless tea last hours. They never buy the sandwiches because they can't chew them and they never buy the cakes because they're not like they used to be. The watchers never pass the time. But they watch the time. Closely. They watch routine and habit and foible and idiosyncrasy. They know what time the lights change from rush hour mode to regular mode, they know how long the old bid with the stick and the dog has to cross once the green man comes on, they know the order in which the cleaner wipes the tables outside the Highcliffe Arms, they know what time the nursery mummies appear with their offspring in the park, and which amusement each child will choose first, and they know exactly who turns up to which bus stop and when.

And, just recently, a new watcher has appeared. And she is not like the other watchers. Not at all like the other watchers. For a start, she is a she. She has an air of prosperity and purpose and she is young. For a watcher, she is young. She wears Viyella, she has all her own teeth, she smiles far too much, she comes alone and she brings a mysterious screen with her. She seems to watch it for long periods of time, routinely sliding her index finger up and down the screen. And then, all of a sudden, she will hold it up to the window and take a photograph with it. The time-passers have no idea what, or whom, she is snapping. She doesn't look like a journalist or a policewoman or a spy. Not that the time-passers would know what a journalist or a policewoman or a spy looks like, unless she were in uniform, or carried an old typewriter, or kept talking into a microphone hidden in her chest. She even has a cake with her pot of tea, on occasion. Fancy bitch. And she annoys the time-passers because she is wantonly and obsequiously polite to Mrs Belton. And Mrs Belton doesn't deserve her kindness because she is fat and rude and loud and she's forever having a dig about them not spending any money in her shop.

It is Thursday and it is approaching ten in the evening. Greasy spoons, of course, are shut at this time of night. Of course they are. All the bread's gone stale, the cakes are stiff and the punters have all gone to the alehouses to get away from their unloved-ones. But not Mrs Benton's. Mrs Benton is always open. Mrs Benton is always open because she is frightened of closing. She is frightened of the silence and the solitude that lurk at the top of the spiral staircase leading to her mucky flat. She is equally frightened of missing the 85p that she'd take from one of the many vagabonds who come loitering around the park fringes at this time of night. So she's always open. Mrs Benton. And they all know that she is always open. So they come. They always come. Just for a bit of warmth and the illusion of company. And this time of night is often her busiest time.

They used to go in the pubs, these hobos. And their scraggy dogs. But now, even the dingiest pubs seem to have bouncers with wires strapped to their faces and straining shirts and crotches and even more tightly wound patience. So they know to stay away. Besides, you can't buy anything in a pub for 85p these days. Not even a packet of crisps.

Now Mrs Viyella does look as though she could stretch to a beer or two, maybe even a cold bottle of Chardonnay. Or two. But she is in again. With her cup of tea. And her stale scone. And her screen. And the three wasters in the corner are all excited because her split-line skirt is revealing a bit of flesh. Pasty, varicosed it may be. But it is flesh. It is female flesh. Just. And it is the nearest they've been to it for some considerable time. One of them even threatens to dig deep for a second cuppa.

So when a young student walks in, all leather and boots and cleavage and earphones, the oldies are unnerved. Silence. Eerie.

'What can a get yer, luv?'

'Tea, please.'

'Mug or cup.'

'How much is a mug?'

'Pound.'

Ellie scrabbles around in her leather jacket.

'There.'

'Milk n sugar?'

'Milk.'

'I'll shout when it's ready, luv.'

'Thanks.'

Ellie is early. And the Doc is going to be late. He texted as she left Pete's. It didn't sound good. He was on his way to hospital or something. She could have stayed at Pete's a bit longer but it all got a bit awkward because he couldn't have sex. No idea what happened. They did what they always did and he seemed up for it when she arrived. But she waited on all fours for ages while he frantically tried to wake the old man. Nothing doing. And he got himself in a bit of a state. So she got dressed, took her weed and left. And in any case, by the time the text came through, she had started walking up Carsley Crescent. And then Jonny went and stuck his great big fuckin nose in and she couldn't go back. So she's got time to kill. Quite a lot of it. In fact, she doesn't know how much time. And what she should do is go home and get some sleep. She's weary. But one of the things making her weary is the situation with the Doc. She needs to finish it. She's bored with his brain and she's bored with his penis and she needs to move on and be a proper student. And it's only a matter of time before he finds out that she is sleeping with someone else and that she has lied to him repeatedly. In fact, he may already know. She has to see him tonight, however long she has to wait. And although she has never been in this shitty caf before, for obvious reasons, one thing she does know is that it never seems to shut. And the fat woman behind the counter will probably stay open for as long as she needs to be there. And she can see the bus stop from here. So she goes in, orders a tea and sits down before she has time to think clearly.

And had she done so, she would have seen that there is a problem with this caf. And the more Ellie thinks about it, the bigger the problem appears. It is not the faint smell of piss or the grubby tables or the mithering old bat behind the counter or the general air of destitution and death. It is not even the sight of a pathetic, lone cherry bakewell whose cherry has slipped onto the body of a bluebottle lying in the gutter of the cake cabinet.

It is one of the other customers. To her right and just in front of her, facing the road that runs right outside the door and through Highcliffe Corner, is someone she recognises. And she is pretty sure that the woman recognises her – the faint flicker of acknowledgement her glance gave away as Ellie approached the glass door was just enough to signal the danger to her. And she nearly turned away. Nearly. But she reacted just a fraction too late and a sudden volte-face would have been an admission of guilt. Ellie is not at all sure of what. But she is sure that it would have given her away in some way. So there she is, seated ever so slightly over the watcher's shoulder. Just sufficiently adrift to mean that this woman would have to act very deliberately to strike up a conversation with her.

For a few minutes, the air is heavy with tension and anticipation. Ellie is trying to mind her own business. But also mind that of the watcher, to see what she is up to, knowing that this woman is only ever up to no good. At least, that's what the Doc always tells her. And the watcher is trying to keep her eye on the bus stop, on the imminent arrival of her prey, but simultaneously keep half an eye on the bait, which is sitting immediately behind her. She is also trying to compute an explanation for this unusual behaviour in the event of a confrontation. Why would a senior member of staff at the local secondary school be idly drinking tea in a dirty old caf at 10.30 at night?

And the time-passers are not sure whether to look at the watcher's partially-uncovered thighs or the youngster's ample cleavage, her heaving youthfulness barely contained by the thinning black top.

And then everything changes. The lights are on red. And a banged-up old student car is revving at the lights, the driver seemingly aggravated and anxious to get somewhere. And Ellie doesn't even need to look through the windscreen to know who is behind the driver's wheel. And she knows exactly where he is going. It's Thursday. The weekend is approaching. That means gigs and parties and women and drugs. And it means pills for the dancing and weed for the sex afterwards. And he has always run out by Thursday. Always. That's why she often sees him at Pete's on a Thursday. That is how she met him. That is how they came to go to Manchester together and to take off one another's clothes in a drug-addled frenzy. She smiles at the thought of that lovely night they had at the Ghostpoet gig. And an utterance of contentedness or joy must have come out of her mouth. Because Viyella turns round quite sharply. And smiles. And then it dawns on Ellie. The smile on Viyella's face. The sarcasm and the sardonic anticipation in that smile wake her from her stupor. Shit. He is going to Pete's. And Jonny the

193

stalker saw her with him in the library on Ghostpoet night. And Jonny gets to know all sorts because he fuckin stalks her all the time and what if he's said somert to Pete? Pete is an angry man and a very possessive man an ee can get very fuckin angry and... shit this is a mess. Shit shit shit.

Ellie waits for the lights to change. The car speeds off. She runs from the caf and across the road. It's quicker across the park. Dark. Foreboding. But much quicker. And she needs to get to Pete's as soon as fuckin possible.

And the only movement Viyella makes as the shop door bangs back on its hinges, is to raise the screen very deliberately up above the line of the central reservation, take aim, and click. Just before Ellie disappears into the foliage of the park trees.

Chapter 35

When Gareth pushes the battered old wooden door of number 117 Carsley Crescent, the first thing he notices is that it is not properly shut. The second is the blood on the carpet at the foot of the stairs. He smells coffee and TCP. He shouts several times as he climbs the worn, woolly stairs. Nothing. Not a sound.

The kitchen. No one. Cascades of dirty pots and cutlery, impromptu ashtrays, decaying pizzas in decaying pizza boxes, half-hung hats and jumpers and a refracted light coming from the street lamp outside. Two giant speakers and a guitar amp of equal disproportion soak up more than their share of surface space to the left. The yellowed linoleum floor is patchy and bitty and the heavily-grained table and chairs are all askew and awry. It's like a fragmented jigsaw puzzle or a disjointed, Dali-esque canvas. And it fuckin stinks. Melted cheese, tomato purée, coffee, burnt toast, ash, weed, matches, damp, mould, mildew, disinfectant. Stale. Just stale, sullied, airless, asphyxiating.

Gareth muffles a cough. The cough of a first-time smoker after inhaling to impress his mates. He stands in the kitchen doorway, completely still. Listening. Listening. There is, of course, someone in the flat. But whoever it is, is either comatose, dead or hovering. Just like him. Or maybe the Police have finally caught up with Mr Verity. Maybe Mr Verity is in cuffs right now, telling the truth. And being told a few home-truths. Or maybe one of his deals has gone tits up and 'the boys' have been to mete out some vigilante justice. Maybe what he saw downstairs was the fringes of a turf war, as the papers

195

amusingly like to call it. Gareth always likes to imagine gangs of spindly, wizened, chisel-jawed ecstasy-heads chucking clumps of grass and rosebuds at one another from behind smouldering bongs on a piece of semi-industrial wasteland somewhere. He'd certainly like to see it. But just at this juncture, he needs to know that he is alone. Or that he is not. But he needs to know.

He turns and cranes his neck into the lounge. Another shit-tip. But no one. So he heads down the corridor. The bulb is out and there is no natural light. He can't even see the door to Pete's room, which is directly in front of him at the end of the corridor.

The bathroom. Toilet unflushed and spotted with drying urine. Showerhead hanging by a thread and rusting in the bath, which is cracked down one side. Towels on the floor and the 1970s, rather plush, double-fronted bathroom cabinet – the kind in which Dad used to keep his Brut and his Old Spice and his badger's arse shaving brush – is gaping. Floss and enough Paracetamol to kill the pain of a jungle-full of elephants. It's unlikely that all the receptacles actually contain Paracetamol, of course. Something much more interesting, of that Gareth is sure. He is equally sure that the diluted stains on the back of the sink and one of the towels is blood. And it looks fresh. The cold tap is dripping and one of the towels is very damp.

Pete's bedroom door. The other two are empty. He knocks, very gently, almost as though he doesn't really want the occupant to hear. If there is one, that is. Nothing. He pushes the handle and opens the door a couple of inches. Feet. Well, boots. The bed is to the right, behind the door and the boots are dangling over the edge of the bed, lifeless. He opens the door fully.

He has never been in Pete's room before. Very few people have ever been afforded access to his little fiefdom. Gareth had imagined it to be in a similar state to the kitchen, only littered with extraordinarily expensive drugs and clothes and the accoutrements of a dealing business, whatever they are. But it is sparse, austere, immaculate. The wardrobe is regimented:

shirts all ironed and hung equidistant, jeans all pressed and each hung with a belt, the shoes are parallel and perpendicular and every one is shaped by an old-fashioned, sprung, wooden retainer. The windowsill is clean and dust-free and displays two polished, black and white photographs. One is of two smiling, loving parents, the other of a lad at his graduation ceremony, smartly suited with cape and mortar board and clutching a ribboned scroll. Gareth smiles. The bedding is Ferrari Formula One bedding. The kind Granny would have bought him for Christmas when he was twelve. Bless.

And Pete is laid all across it. He is fully clothed in Fila and Henri Lloyd, as ever, and he looks warm, cosy, contented. Except that his face and his jugular and his sternum and the front-upper of his clothes are all soaked in very deep, dark blood. The blood isn't running anymore and it isn't pooling. It's now soaking into every crevasse created by the body-shape and the bed. Poor old Ferrari is redder than it once was. And Gareth doesn't know whether to laugh or cry, run or call an ambulance, sit and comfort him or steal a few pills from the stash.

'Hello. Hellooo. Anyone in?'

Gareth recognises the voice instantly. Shit shit shit shit shit shit. Fuck. Fuck. Gareth turns round and bestrides the threshold of Pete's room, caught in the half-light. And she is stood at the end of the corridor. Still. Completely still. Save the butterfly flickering of the eyelashes, adjusting to the darkness, and the gently palpitating chest. And she is framed in the aperture, palpable, profound, yet vague, like a gossamer black and white photograph. The faded light coming in from the kitchen illuminates her gothish demeanour perfectly: the menacing tenebrosity of her eyes and her jet, scrimped hair, set against the pale, deathly blanche of her complexion; the blood-red lips pouting; and the fullness of her figure exuding sex and deviance in this very confined space. Fuck she's gorgeous. She really is. Gareth, on the other hand, is in near blackness, just a few chinks of light from Pete's offset window catching his lower limbs. In this blind alley, his stature is all-consuming.

197

And she knows exactly who she is looking at. The aura is primatial, brooding, carnal. In a word, it is poise. And Ellie thinks she is probably in love with him.

And just as the adulterous tension nears violence, just as two people are forced to stare at their own weaknesses, their own fetid, fetishist, fornicating flaws, just as she looks into him and sees herself sucking voraciously on another's spewing cock or opening herself right up, fingering relentlessly, just as he looks into her and sees himself grinding his hips into another's cunt and grinding his jaw into the flesh. Just at that moment, there is an invidious yet overwhelming affection. There is an utterly vituperative love.

'Fancy a brew?'

Her words echo down the corridor. She seems to have been there for hours.

'That be nice.'

And he walks towards her, slowly, expecting that she will turn into the kitchen to negotiate the detritus of Pete's domestics and of her relationship with this beautiful man. But she doesn't. She does not move. At all. She wants to wait. Just a moment. Just long enough to see the whites of his eyes. To see who is left inside the shell she has just stared down. He will stop. Of course he will. Just beyond arm's length. Just at that teetering edge between complicity and intimacy.

But he doesn't. He slows. He comes right into her world. He stops. He hovers just for a second. And the long, loping wings extend outwards and envelope her. Ever so gently. The mohair of his gilet just caressing the leather of her jacket.

She moves in. Just an inch or two.

'I'm sorry. I'm so sorry. I wasn't ready for this. When you came, I just wasn't ready for it.'

He's not sure what she means. But, right now, the human warmth is all that matters.

'Me neither. Neither was I.'

He draws back. They look hard into one another's eyes.

'The kitchen is a fuckin shithole. Shall we go in here?'

She takes his hand and draws him into one of the bedrooms. She closes the door. She takes off her clothes. Slowly, deliberately but perfunctorily. And he does the same. They spoon into one another under a single white sheet. And Ellie is soon asleep. Gareth paws at her shoulders for a while and pushes his semi-erect penis into her bum. But he's tired too. And this is not the time. This is reconciliation. It comes without condition. And he's just happy to be with her. At least, for now.

Chapter 36

If Jonny hadn't got an erection, it wouldn't have happened. If Jonny hadn't been so neat and tidy and just-so, none of it would have happened. If Jonny had locked the door when Gareth left. And gone for a lie down, like he said he would. It would not have been like this.

If Jonny had just eaten his food. Grandad always said you should eat your food up. And Grandad knows many things. Grandad is the cleverest man Jonny knows. He must be because he reads lots of thick books and he knows lots of strange words and he used to be a Headmaster and Headmasters are the most intelligent people in school. They must be, otherwise how do they get to be Headmasters? The clue is in the title, stupid. HEADmaster. The others are just masters. Teachers who know about one particular subject. But the HEADmaster knows about all the subjects. Mathematics, Physics, Geography. All of them. And he has to do all the other things too, like make sure the boys' changing rooms are clean and the toilets are flushed and the windows are closed and the whiteboards are scrubbed last thing at night. And the grass is cut on the fields and the goalposts are taken down in summer.

Sometimes Jonny has to think carefully when Grandad is talking to him because he uses big words, or just different words. For instance, Jonny doesn't have a Headmaster. Jonny has a Headteacher. At first Jonny would ask Grandad what a Headteacher does and Grandad would get irritated because he said that the politicos had got hold of the education system and now they were appropriating the English Language and had decided that Headmaster was too pompous and aloof and it set an air of authority and distance between pupils and masters which was no longer wanted. Masters were intelligent people with knowledge and wisdom to impart. And now teachers are just pupils' friends and babysitters and they teach them no more than Mum and Dad could do straight from a book or a newspaper. And Jonny didn't really understand politicos or appropriating or pompous or aloof. He did understand pupils but thought it a bad word and Grandad would get irritated again. So he stopped asking. But when he joked that we all need aloof over our heads, Grandad lightened up a bit and chuckled. He likes plays on words, does Grandad. Or *jeux de mots*. He uses other languages quite a lot does Grandad – master of all his subjects, see. Headmaster.

And now look at him. Head of nothing. Sitting lonely on a park bench, no clue where he is or what's just happened. An alien. A sad, lonely, confused and misunderstood old git. And he doesn't even have the dog to comfort him, just some bonkers old bloke putting his hand over his shoulder and talking to him like he's a child. A pupil, even.

If only Gareth hadn't left in such a hurry. The kitchen was in a terrible state. Food burning, water over-boiling, raw asparagus all over the surface. And the cooker looked as though it hadn't seen a cloth in months. And the cleaning fluid was so old and unused it had crusted over. And Jonny simply cannot deal with mess. He cannot leave things unfinished, undone, half-baked. He has to have closure. Otherwise, he cannot move on. The food was half-prepared. So he couldn't eat it cos it wasn't ready but he couldn't finish preparing it either because someone else had started it. And in any case, he couldn't cook in that mess. The hob hadn't been cleaned since the day Sean moved in and he was never going to do the asparagus on that. And Gareth had cut the tips too short anyway. And even assuming he had been able to finish the cooking, he wouldn't have been able to eat off that table, with its junk food and drugs and random books lying all over it. Crumbs from 19 bloody 75 or something.

So Jonny didn't go for a lie down, like he'd said he would. Jonny found a clean cloth and a brush and he cleaned and he tidied and he scrubbed and he sorted and he sided and he didn't stop until the kitchen was pristine. Pristine. And it felt good. It felt good because this was cleaning night. This was the night of the big cleansing. This was the night when Jonny was going to straighten everything, clean everything, tidy everything. This was the night when the bastards who had been screwing his beloved girl were going to confront their misogyny and destroy one another. This was the night when Derek was going to be saved from himself. This was the night when that bitch Wilhelm was going to be outfoxed and outdone and left exposed, naked, flagrant, humiliated.

It was all clean. It was all tidy. It was all ready. It was all set up. It was all prepared.

About half an hour. About half an hour and Jonny will start walking steadily but surely towards Highcliffe Corner. About half an hour and Dr Ramsbottom will pull up at the bus stop in the usual way. And Wilhelm will be waiting. In the greasy spoon. With her lens primed. But Ellie will not get in. Ellie will tell the Doc that she does not want to see him anymore and that she will not be meeting him from now on. And the Doc will drive off alone, to the sound of Wilhelm's camera clicking evidence of absolutely nothing, images of no consequence whatever. And all the while, Gareth and Pete will be kicking ten bells out of one another in Carsley Crescent. And Jonny will follow Ellie from the park back to that road. Carefully. At a distance. And when she emerges from Pete's flat, when she comes out of that den of iniquity, looking like a ghost, Jonny will be the poet to lull her into the warmth of his embrace, the love of his heart. He will be her real Ghostpoet. And he will take her back to his house. The house that is now cleansed of its devil. And soon, Mummy will come home and they'll put on some ambient house music or pile-driving rock and jump around the kitchen together until they all fall about laughing. And Jonny will take Ellie to his bedroom and spoon with her all night, under his posters of Stephen Patrick Morrissey and Robert Smith.

Jonny rocks back on the kitchen chair, admiring his handy work. Waiting. Waiting.

Through the sash window, Plan B has been achieving fame and fortune, going on a bender, having casual sex, indicted for rape, doing time, finding God and desperately trying to make up for lost time. In other words, living out an entire life in 50 minutes. He has also been helping Jonny clean. It is almost as though Musicman knows what's going on in other people's lives. Plan B is a bloke who wrote an album called *The Defamation of Strickland Banks*. It is a concept album and it is a quite outstanding, beautifully-constructed tale of a slighted pop-star who loses control of his ego and pays with his freedom and his sanity. And yet his personality emerges from the album with some redemption – he is open, wilful, loving, stoical and warm, though terribly flawed. It is a very human story of spiritual absolution. And the real beauty in this album, the real visceral power lies in the fact that this emotional rollercoaster on which we are taken lends itself to powerful musical genres, from heart-rending ballads to vicious, hedonistic rap. The musical journey plays out in tandem with the sentimental one, tempting us to forgive even the most clichéd lyrical and musical aspects of the album.

Gareth could so easily have been Mr Strickland Banks. Oh, he's nothing like Mr Banks in background or social class. But a hedonist is a hedonist. And even hedonists fall in love. Then what do they do? They do what Gareth does. They destroy. They kick and they flail and they fuck up. They fight everything and everyone, not realising that the person they really need to fight is in the mirror. Jonny feels sorry for Gareth. He likes him. And he's been lovely to Sean. But now Jonny has closed the sash in order to wipe it free of the grease that has been running down it for months. And Musicman has moved on to some US rapper who is shouting nigger and motherfucker and bitch and other gratuities. Jonny is glad to have closed the window.

Knock on the door. Jonny stills himself. Knock knock. If he stays silent, it'll go away. Shush. Knock knock. The door handle drops and the door eases ajar.

'Hello. Hello. Anyone in? Only me. Hello.'

Jonny sees the tits. Then the blonde bob. Then the heels.

'Oh ello. Has Garyboy gone out?'

Jonny is utterly without the power of speech.

'Sorry. I didn't mean to frighten you. I just left my Nano in Gaz' bedroom. Errm. Do you mind if I go and get it?'

Jonny nods nervously. She hesitates.

'Are you ok?... You sure?... You don't look well at all. Are you ok?'

She drops her baggage and clomps into the kitchen. The wound at the back of his head is apparent. Sticky hair, matted blood. Stitches.

'Oh ma God. What happened to you? This just happened? What av yer done, our kid? As our Gaz left you in this state? What the hell?'

Jonny feels compelled to defend himself. Or his friends. Or something.

'It's fine. It's fine, really. I just fell off a barstool and cracked my head. I went to hospital and they stitched me up. I'm fine. I just need to rest. That's all. Really, I'm fine.'

'Did Gaz not tell you? I'm a nurse. At the hospital. And he shouldn't have left you alone with concussion, now should he? Everyone knows that you don't leave a concussed patient alone.'

She leans over the wound and gently moves aside the hair to get a closer look. Her flesh is close. Very. Jonny has never seen a pair of tits this close before. And the stroking of his scalp doesn't help either. She has soft hands. Jonny is tired as it is. It's like a pornographic lullaby. Breasts, head massage, slight concussion, after-effects of MDMA. Jonny feels a bit faint. He puts his hands out to steady himself and he feels her hips. She is slender, they are sensual. Jonny holds tight.

'Alright? Are you ok? Does that hurt? There's going to be a lot of bruising there for a while. You need to take care. What's your name?'

'Jonny.'

Jonny is faint. He lolls forward onto her breasts. And she has not the slightest hesitation in keeping him close. She doesn't seem at all uncomfortable with this intimacy.

'Jonny what?'

'Hainsworth.'

'Oh. You must be Sean's brother. Hello, I'm Karen. People call me Kaz. Are you ok, Jonny?'

'Ok. Yes. I'm ok. Just tired.'

Jonny's eyes are heavy. Very.

'Where is Gaz? Do you know?'

'He's gone to settle a score with his dealer. They both bin seein the same woman n the shit's gonna hit the fan.'

Kaz stops rubbing his scalp. She holds him on the jawline and pulls his head up to hers. There's a tear in one of her eyes. Like she knew but had never admitted it to herself. Gareth is Gareth. It doesn't take long to work him out.

'Come on, Jonny. We need to get you to bed. I'll sit with you awhile.'

And that is why Jonny is late. That is why Jonny doesn't get to the park in time. That is why he is running so hard. That is why he calls out so desperately for her to turn round and watch for the car coming at her... Gareth told him to lock the door. He told him. Jonny always does as he is told. But now Jonny is standing in Sean's room, having all his clothes carefully removed by Nurse Karen, who is intent on tucking him up. Even though she has just been told that her lover is a duplicitous bastard who has probably passed on some sexual infection to her. Even though her instinct is to run out the house and down to the nearest pub for a cry and a vodka n orange. Nurse Karen has done this many times now. And so she removes his shirt and his string vest all too quickly and before Jonny can do or say anything, she is drawing the jeans and the pants, in one, down over his thighs.

And there it is. Proud, poised, primed.

And Nurse Karen must have known before she started sliding down the jeans. She must have. She must have thought about that bastard Gareth and how innocent and sweet and lovely Jonny was and how he needed mothering and how that bastard Gareth had wanted anal sex and she'd refused and so he'd denied her any at all and she'd really wanted to feel a man inside her tonight. And Jonny had been so ready. So very ready. Tonight he was going to clean everything, clean everyone. The kitchen was done. Plan B was like a sign from the gods. It was all set up. Tonight he would spoon with Ellie and it would all be nice. Clean. Tidy. And now he is late. He is very late. And he is sticky and sweaty and uncomfortable. And Nurse Karen is in Sean's bed. And the sheets aren't clean. And she doesn't have a key to lock up. And Jonny's head is bursting, burgeoning. And he can't run fast enough to clear it.

Chapter 37

Ellie kisses him awake.

Gareth is dozing, dreaming. He is having a waking dream in which he is stuck in a pub, drinking with people he dislikes. He seems to be buying every round and yet every time he leans forward to drink, his pint glass has gone. He keeps contributing to the conversation but no one is listening to him and even when he deliberately makes contentious points, everyone just picks up on the previous comment. And what is really strange is that he is starting to slur his words and feel light-headed and a bit delirious. And everyone else is sober. Stone-cold sober. But every time he gets up to leave, they beg him to stay for just one more. And he ends up at the bar ordering four, five, six pints of some pokey real ale whose name is probably a euphemism for vagina, or dirty sex or drugs. And Gareth doesn't even drink the bloody stuff. And then he sits back down to be ignored and ridiculed all over again.

'I think Pete's up... Gareth, I think Pete's up... are you awake?'

Ellie is whispering but Gareth hears her perfectly well. At first he's still in the dream and Ellie has maybe come to rescue him from this shallow nightmare. He smiles to himself.

'Gareth. What do we do?'

Her whisper is louder. He opens one eye. Her make-up is a bit smudged and her hair is all shocked to one side of her head.

'You've got lippy on your face, Gareth. Quite suits you.'

She kisses him. Properly. Heavy footsteps are padding about and pots are clanking in the kitchen. Pete is swearing to himself asthmatically. And Gareth bolts upright. Wide awake.

She called him Gareth. Gareth. And as he is about to say something – not that he has any idea what is about to come out, as he is about to utter some shite, she covers his mouth with her hand. Completely. The sudden shoulder movement pushes her tits together and Gareth gets a rush of blood. He starts to kiss the fleshy cleavage. But she draws his chin back up and mouths 'sshhh' without a sound leaving her voice-box. Pete's footsteps have quietened to a tiptoe and he's right outside the door. Hovering. Listening. From one nightmare to another. Fuck.

A few minutes pass by. The air hangs heavy. Stillness. Silence. All three are holding their breath for just the slightest noise. Tick tock. Tick tock. A tap is dripping somewhere. Maybe outside. Gareth is annoyed. He's annoyed that Pete is disturbing his sex life – he's just wholly in the mood to fuck Ellie right now. Hard, carnal, almost brutal. And he's pretty sure she's up for it too. And annoyed because he can't sit Ellie up and explain all the shit about his name and the deceit and the fact that he didn't realise he would fall in love with her and, yes, at first he just fancied her and wanted to see her body and put another notch on the bedpost under 'Goth'. But then he realised and he's sorry and he really wants to see her again and be with her and… And it doesn't occur to him that a heartfelt, sincere, grovelling explanation is not necessarily conducive to bestial sex. The arrogance is delightful and youthful and almost charming in its naivety. Or it would be, if Ellie had any interest in what is going through his head right now.

And then Pete sniffs loudly and bounds down the stairs. The door unhinges. And slams only a second later. They both listen. Are two people coming back up the stairs? Or has Pete gone out? No sound. A few more minutes stroke by on the old ticker by the bed. Is this a trap? Is Pete skulking? Waiting? Fuck knows. Ellie gets up. Suddenly all business and purpose and logic. She reaches for her clothes. Gareth watches her as she bends.

'Beautiful fanny, Ell.'

'Gareth, we need to get out of here. If he comes back and we're still here, he'll fuckin maim the pair of us. While he's out we need to go.'

'Come back to bed, Ell. Let me taste you. Please. It seems ages.'

'Gareth. Please. I'm scared an Pete can be fuckin violent when he's angry. I need to go.'

'From what I hear, you'd know, Ell.'

She turns suddenly and glares at him. She needs to shout so many fuckin things at him but she can't. Not now.

'You've got a great body, Ell. It's just perfect for sex. Come 'ere.'

Ellie ignores him and carries on getting dressed.

'You know the mark of real beauty, Ell?'

She struggles with her bra strap.

'It's people who look better naked than clothed.'

She stares down the mirror and licks her fingers to tidy up the eyeliner and the lippy. It's all a bit hopeless but she just needs to leave.

'You look gorgeous in all your gothy paraphernalia. But you look even better with nothing on.'

'Gareth, for fucksake. You do what you want. But I'm goin.'

'Ell. Ell. Come back to bed. Let's be rude for a bit. Who gives a fuck about Pete. I'll sort Pete.'

But his voice strains to reach her as she exits the room and heads for the stairwell. The door slams shut.

'Fuck. Fuck. Fuck. How's she know my name? What the fuck?'

A few minutes later, when Gareth pushes the gas on his silly old Civic and does a screeching U-turn on Carsley Crescent, he notices two things: one, he has fuck-all fuel in the tank and, two, Ellie must have run across the park because, had she gone up Carsley, she wouldn't have cleared the top by now and he'd be able to see her. He puts his foot to the floor.

Pete waits a matter of seconds, engages his 1.8 injection engine, and does precisely the same manoeuvre. Just a bit quicker.

Chapter 38

He is sitting on one of the park benches. He is facing the wrong way. Or the right way. If he had come for a night-time view of the daffodils and the rusty swings n slides, that is. The roundabout is crying to a stop and the squirrels are starting at every flicker and flinch of life. It is well beyond sundown but the night is crepuscular. It has only half-reclaimed the day and nature's nocturnals are tentative in their encroachment. Urbanity is sliding into a sleep that never quite descends and the hum of human invention is but a soundtrack to silence, like a buzzing fridge in a vacant mezzanine townhouse.

Marjory loved this park. At least, the back of the bench declares such on its rusted plaque. Yet another modern, facile evocation of intangible sentiment, nullified by its very public proclamation, he would no doubt have, well, proclaimed.

Dr Ramsbottom wonders how many people passing this way knew of Marjory. He wonders if her love for this verdant urbanity stemmed from loneliness, from a simple desire for inner peace, or from a memory of nascent love and companionship. For sure, by the time her affection had been etched into this oak, she had long gone. A headstone to happiness.

But not for the old boy on the bench. He is grumpy. From behind his supplicant shoulders, Dr Ramsbottom can see the jabbering jowls and the digital gesticulation. He is berating. But he is alone. Or maybe he knows he is there.

'Four across: harsh, unfeeling, unsentimental. It's ASPERGIC… but then seven down doesn't fit. Bloody fool. I used to whizz through this in a tea-break.'

'ASPERITY. ASPERGIC is not in the *Shorter Oxford*, I think you'll find. Sir.'

Dr Ramsbottom lurches into his world. The old lad is not the slightest startled by his intrusion.

'Hello there, Doc. Did you say ASPERITY?'

'Yes I did. And how are you, sir?'

'Well I'm annoyed but it's nice of you to help me out. I've spent my life finishing other people's sentences and now an alumnus is damn-well finishing mine. And not for the first time tonight.'

'Maybe Marjory would have known the answer.'

'Marjory? Who to goodness is Marjory? I never taught a girl by that name.'

'Never mind, Mr Mayfield, are you alright?'

'Yes of course, my dear. Nothing to worry about. I just get a little vexed at times, you know. Old age, I suppose. I am permitted the odd outburst, am I not? In any case, since when did you address me as Mr Mayfield?'

'Of course, sir. Of course you are.'

He draws a long breath.

'It's just that… well… you have been involved in an accident, Mr Mayfield, and I am not sure you realise the severity of the situation.'

'Have I? What the Devil has become of me? Am I gone to the other side? Am I in a state of shameful delirium? Am I bloodied and bowed? What is it? Is that why I am Mr Mayfield all of a sudden?'

It is then that Dr Ramsbottom notices the leather strap wrapped around his right wrist.

'Mr Mayfield. If I may, what is that, sir?'

'Well what a ridiculous question, dear boy. For one whose lexicon includes the word *asperity*, your powers of deduction are rather lacking. Why, it's a simple leather dog-lead, of course.'

'I know, Mr Mayfield. I know.'

Dr Ramsbottom is shivering. His heart has just gone horribly cold.

'Sir, is your dog an old English Sheepdog with one white ear?'

'Yes indeed, dear. You know very well that it is.' Mafe is agitated. But the thought of Sheppie immediately calms him.

'Sheppie is only a young thing and she does get a little playful at times. Funny, though. They get under your skin very quickly, don't you find? Is it the loyalty, the joyful obedience, or simply those eyes? Eyes whose supplication belies an almost vicious diligence.'

Mafe hadn't heard the screech of tyres. He hadn't heard the thud of chassis on concrete. He hadn't heard the lightning crack of pane or the mitraille of metal ripping the bark from the heart of the old oak. And then the heart from the bark. Dogs always whimper in films, don't they? Shep hadn't. The hit was too fast, too hard. And too true. Gareth Simpson was thrown clear. But Shep wasn't.

And had Mafe looked up from his crossword, he would have seen Jackson Pollock on Nature's own canvas – the beautiful, vibrant yellow of the daffodil bed, which had become a temporary resting place, flecked with lifeless red. And had he not been numbed by the search for asperity, he would have felt the molten, red liquid running through his knuckle-beds, slowly tap-tapping onto the soft leather of the severed lead. And had he turned his head through 90 degrees to the right, he would have seen the girl, that girl, hobbling hurriedly, clutching her right shoulder, dripping, ushering her autistic stalker into the night, he would have seen her lover's nemesis straddling the central reservation, clutching a screen, and running stealthily away and over Highcliffe Moor, as his grandson had done just a few nights ago, and he would have seen the bastard with whom she was utterly besotted, lying dead in the flowers, his battered old Honda Civic wedged into the old oak tree of Highcliffe Corner. But he would not have seen the other car, all spoilers and tints and blackouts and dangly paraphernalia, accelerating up the park road and into a distant suburb. It was all too fast and too violent for Mr Mayfield.

'We need to take you home, Mr Mayfield.'

'I know, dear. I know. But, you see, I have to make sure Shep's mess is cleared up. The sign tells me I'll be fined up to £1,000, you see. It's not fair to leave dog-mess here. There are children playing, you know.'

'I know, Mr Mayfield. I know. We'll do that for you, Mr Mayfield. We'll do that. You need to rest.'

Mafe stares hard into Dr Ramsbottom's lachrymal lines. Puppy dog, he thinks.

It is dark. Mafe can't see the clues anyway now. So he makes for home.

Marjory loved it here. It says so. A headstone to happiness.

END